For Mike
and
Hilary Moorcock

Contents

Road, *n.* A strip of land along which one may pass from where it is too tiresome to be to where it is futile to go.

Ambrose Bierce,
The Enlarged Devil's Dictionary

Prologue

Wendover stood shivering in the grey dawn, gazing mournfully over the parapet of the flyover: a small, bony man wearing a thin inadequate raincoat. His fingers were stiff, his eyes watering. A light wind interfered with his brown scruffy hair. He had been up all night, watching the cars.

In the uncertain light there was something harsh and inhuman about the landscape, as if the road had been built not for men but for something alien and unguessable; something, perhaps, with steel and ferroconcrete limbs. He half-expected it to appear at any time, striding south, the land groaning under its seven-league steps, but it did not come, and the road stretched away, quiescent: a kinked perspective of grey macadam filmed with a faint sheen of moisture.

It was patched and scarred by short-term repairs, crumbling where carriageway met hard shoulder. Isolated spears of twitch-grass showed at its edges. Cars hummed towards him, Dopplered away north and south.

His cold, free-wheeling mind invested each abrupt, attenuated drone with an inflection of loneliness. Subjective time between the appearance of each car dragged out immeasurably, although in most cases the interval could have been no more than three or four minutes. Occasionally, a gaggle of vehicles would hurtle past below him, dicing for position at speed. At these times Wendover would wince and draw a little way back from the rail. As yet there had been no accident.

Above and behind him stretched the fence. Supported by tapering pillars of concrete at thirty-yard intervals, the pale barriers of chain-link moaned in the wind like an immense musical instrument. At each side of the road they rose forty feet beyond the top level of the cutting, then arced over to meet above the central reservation, eighty or ninety feet above the tarmac. The effect was of a huge cage, the chicken-wire run of an experimental rat maze.

Constructed some years before – by the Fairbairn Coalition, the first administration to face the reality of the disaster – the fence had been a misguided attempt to contain accident effects and protect the urbanized sections of the motorway from damage. In practice it had merely aggravated the incidence of multi-vehicle pile-ups. The Fairbairn government had collapsed noisily in the poor nineties, and none of its successors had hazarded the expense of removing the great metal alleys.

The millennium as a rat cage, thought Wendover sourly: And the word 'accident' is a euphemism. The rats continued to run, whining fixatedly from horizon to horizon.

Wendover's eyes widened. He licked his chapped lips. Travelling north in the high nineties, a black and gold Lewis/Phoenix Sunbird touched the ill-defined periphery of the central reservation. Its driver, feeling his offside wheels contact coarse grass and loose grit, panicked.

Wendover panicked with him. Over-corrected, the Sunbird lurched towards the hard shoulder, the note of its turbine descending rapidly. A second over-correction. The car traced an 80mph sine curve for a mile, then hit the reservation again. Blood warmed Wendover's lips. This time it took off, performing a slow, deadly barrel-roll.

Its doors flew open, ejecting a small, whirling puppet. A faint cry, hardly audible above the scream of the racing turbine. Then it was down in the south-bound lanes, slewing across the path of a sixty-ton wagon. There was a painful mewl of tyres as the heavy rig jack-knifed, rolled, and leapt towards the nearside of the cutting, shedding things. It climbed the embankment and slammed into the fence.

A single vibrant note boomed into the dawn air as the taut chainlink took up the massive strain, reverberated, and threw the vehicle back into the road. Its fuel tanks exploded with a numbing basso rumble, spraying blazing JP4 across an acre of tarmac.

Wendover stopped yelling and closed his mouth.

He shook his head like a man coming out of a hypnagogic vision, and turned away, his eyes staring and hysterical, yet unfocused. He stumbled down to the slip road and struck out east for home. He was cold, the November morning had penetrated his raincoat. It had begun to drizzle, a fine, chill mist.

Behind him, the two-tone wail of the Clearance vehicles made a minor chord with the still-vibrating fence – a keening and dismal threnody. He shivered. He tried to whistle a drab little counterpoint to the death music, tried to believe the accident had numbed his emotions as well as his mind, and that he hadn't waited all night long for just such an occurrence.

But Wendover was fascinated by the sickness of his world, and his red-knuckled hands were locked together, as if by proximity they might gain some sort of comfort.

*

Prologue

In this region the motorway environs were predominantly agricultural — wide sweeps of dark plough separated from low-lying pasture land by stark thorn hedges, patched here and there with leafless spinneys and fox-coverts. Rooks planed overhead like ragged machines.

Wendover had a small practice in a village about a mile from the flyover. It poked out of the farmland like a geological mistake, perpetually surprising the surrounding fields. The utilitarian/rural: a grey Norman church; shops with frontages thirty years out of date; a graveyard that seemed always to be sliding into the river; drab red brick, and the rare timbered façade. There were three streets. A number of lanes wound off into the patchwork of fields. Sometimes there were swans on the river, usually there were moorhens with long ungainly legs and bright beaks. By the church, elms grew from an eyot that split the smooth unhurried water. By the time Wendover reached its outskirts, the place was beginning to face the certainty of another day.

It straggled blearily out of the morning at him: a thin wisp of smoke, a chintz curtain lifted briefly as he passed; a dog barking, a white face, a muted cough. In the main street a fat man was delivering milk.

As Wendover passed him, they exchanged wary glances. Wendover nodded. The milkman averted his face with a peculiar little duck of the head. It was not an uncommon occurrence.

Two big chestnut horses, each with forelegs crêpe-bandaged, clattered out of the gates of the hunt stable, led by a hunched girl groom in a faded flannel shirt. The warm smell of horse. Her eyes scraped at him from the mask of an acne he could do nothing to cure. (She had mumbled gruffly, something about a boy. Making this last plea, she was pathetically scruffy. And he, safe behind the surgery desk, spreading his arms in a gesture of ineffectuality. It would have been easier to help had she cracked her skull in a fall.)

SOVIETS ACCUSE USA. He trudged past the newsagent's shop, where they were taking delivery of the morning editions. Newsprint fluttered damply in the wind. Water pearled the windscreen of the delivery van. PROMINENT SCIENTISTS SUGGEST.

He bought several papers and a packet of cigarettes, walked on, trying to read and light a cigarette simultaneously. ACCIDENT FIGURES RELEASED. Crossing the river, he was startled by a motor-cycle: it bellowed over the crest of the bridge and became briefly airborne, all engine and savagely raked handlebars. A farm labourer late for work, driving suicidally fast, his face closed and shuttered behind goggles and scarf. His vicious slipstream tore at the newspapers.

Prologue

GOVERNMENT: NEW MEASURES. He cut a swathe of spray through the village. Faintly, Wendover heard the stable girl screaming abuse at him.

Wendover lived in the only modern house in the village.

He would have preferred to use his predecessor's surgery, a big, morose, square building surrounded by conifers like dark, living flames. Three years ago the idea of shutting himself away behind the tall, pebble-faced walls with the river ghosting past the crumbling staithe at the end of the garden had greatly appealed to him, but his wife had insisted on the bright sprawling bungalow, and he had slowly grown used to it.

Built – and he was never to grow used to this – with Vanessa's money, it had a shoddy, spurious air; he constantly expected to find that, like the buildings of Elstree and Hollywood, it was nothing but a façade propped up by timbers – coloured cardboard over flimsy lath. Stone-painted in yellow-ochre, with contrasting woodwork and huge picture windows, it sat uneasily among professionally tailored flower-beds and rockeries. The river pastures mocked it with sombre shades of green; straggling thorn; and the coarse cries of rooks.

Vanessa's snobbery had turned a gentle irony on her: a mile away, beyond a thin frieze of trees, the heavy plant of a construction company ground the earth bare and flat to receive the foundations of an overspill development; where the bungalow had previously had the dubious distinction of being different, it would now be only one of a series of bright rabbit hutches.

Doubtless Vanessa would demand that they move back into the old surgery.

Wendover walked up the red asphalt drive, stopping to run his fingers along the wet flank of Vanessa's pale green turbine car and gaze pensively at the rain misting across the vista of fields. He took his patience in both hands and went in.

After the dawn cold, the centrally heated interior was like a greenhouse.

Vanessa was in the double bedroom, sitting before the big ornate mirror of the dressing table. Wendover realized with a bitterness he no longer wanted to suppress that he rarely saw her face outside the confining frame of the mirror. Deeply frightened by the outbreaks of skin disease that had followed the increases in radiation, she sat for hours in minute examination of her features, applying a bewildering variety of toners and conditioning creams.

The vanity was calculated. Vanessa's body was a lever, a rudimentary machine: without the perfect skin, the smooth, high-cheekboned features, the pretty eyes, it would no longer function. Depressed by the honest admission of something he had known all along, Wendover sat on the bed, feeling the night's weariness overtake him.

She said nothing for a minute, occupied by an intent study of her left temple. She sat easily on the vanity stool, her angular back bare but for the white narrow strip of brassière and the waistband of a tight support brief. Her skin was creamy and pleasant. The muscles beneath tensed as she prepared to notice him.

She abandoned a pink cleansing tissue with an over-brisk gesture that suggested nervousness, turned her attention to his mirror image. Her eyes were direct, blue, disconcerting. They gave an impression of depth.

'Do get up off the bed, Clement. Your coat's all wet.'

For three years her voice had chipped away at his nerves – a reflex of her Cheltenham upbringing, pointing up his inadequacy. Now she injected it with a precise measure of patience, as if she were addressing a bad child. He knew the game. There would be a quarrel, and she would remain urbane, while he shouted hoarsely at the Vanessa he was sure must be in there somewhere; automatically, his churlishness would cast her in the role of injured party. But he had spent the night watching the symptoms of a degenerating world; the system was breaking up, showing the weaknesses at its seams; and a sense of urgency filled him. There was very little time left for playing bedroom scenes.

She said: 'I waited up for you, but you didn't come in.'

Again, the simple, patient indictment. She had returned to the cleansing tissue, sweeping it in long strokes down one cheek. Her hand was steady. She was only limbering up.

'I was out walking. Vanessa, I'm selling the practice. I decided last night. It's not going to mean anything when the collapse comes. I'd rather have it in hard cash now.'

There was a pause. Caught off balance, she was trying to digest the information.

They had discussed it before. Plainly, things were in a state of flux: it would be a good deal safer to have easily convertible assets while the country went through its unavoidable period of political and economic chaos. But Vanessa needed the ancillaries of the age as much as she needed her body, and possibly for the same reasons.

'Clement, when *are* you going to grow up?'

A tinselly laugh. She had got the measure of him.

'Do go and get some sleep, darling. You have a surgery at nine. Please try to look at it sensibly for once: if you don't want to face pimply farm girls with menstrual problems, then don't; but you must find a better excuse than that. An honest one. When this nonsense blows over, you're going to look an incredible fool . . .'

She swivelled round to face him, folding her arms under her breasts so that the cleavage stood out firmly. It was bad tactics. He found himself studying the reflection of her shoulders in the mirror, actually embarrassed. He got up and walked to the door.

'We've got beyond that, Vanessa. Take your own advice. You're hiding behind a concept of life ten years out of date. The system is fragmenting. Everything is changing, and we need the money while it still has buying power. It's no use to us tied up in the practice. We need a different kind of security now; in a few years we'll be scavengers and drifters; a little forethought could help us immensely. Stocks of food . . .'

But she wasn't listening. The pink tissue whispered against her skin. He harshened his voice, but hardly expecting it to get through.

'We need to get away somewhere and ride it out. When people realize this is the finish for the twentieth century they're going to explode. You'll have to learn to do without face . . .'

'Oh, for *God's sake*, Clement! Can't you see I'm busy? Go to bed, go to hell, anything, so long as you leave me alone!'

This rising steadily to a crescendo on *alone*. In the mirror her face twisted and crumpled, spots of colour forming high up on her cheeks. The glass was flecked with little specks of spittle.

'This is real, Vanessa. You can't shout it away.' Moving into the kitchen, he put the boot in hard: 'And stop messing with your face. You can't do anything when the ulcers appear. And you can't prevent it.' Escapist, he thought. Bloody escapist.

In the kitchen he took off the wet raincoat, lit a cigarette, set about making himself a cup of coffee. Refuge in domesticity. The percolator muttered to itself. He inspected his stubbled, hollow-eyed image in the mirror she had installed above the sink; it looked back at him questioningly; he had never enjoyed hurting her before. Nor had he ever succeeded so well. You live with someone, and they're open to you. Bed confidences as weapons. The sobbing that filtered from the bedroom modulated from self-pity to genuine sorrow, supposing there is a difference. Vanessa was losing her parameters.

He managed to ignore the noise for a few minutes, warming his hands over the percolator and thinking of the cold sounds of the Clearance vehicles. Then he carried two cups of coffee into the bedroom.

She was huddled over a *Times* leader which suggested circumspectly that the great reservoir of suicide-prones be prevented from holding licences to drive. Her body was bent uncomfortably; her eyes were red rimmed, her knuckles white at the edges of the paper. Wendover put the coffee on the dressing table. She ignored it.

'I'm sorry,' he said, echoing a hundred other confrontations. 'There's no point in quarrelling.'

Finding no hint of a cure, no hope of a solution, she let the paper slip from her knees. The blue eyes glittered.

'*Here's* an end to it,' she said, upper lip curling away from her sharp teeth: 'If you go on this way, I shall leave you.

'You're an oaf, a bloody clown. You can't come to terms with life, and you're looking for a cheap let-out. You're an oaf. *There's* an end to all the bickering. Go on like this, and we're finished.'

'But . . .' Awareness of his own ineffectuality closed his mouth. He really wasn't in her league.

She drank the coffee quickly, with an expression of distaste. Then she stood up and stepped out of the support brief, leaned forward to undo the fastening of the brassière. She smiled. Then she lay on the bed and spread her legs.

'You'd better have me, Clement. Because if you continue this silliness, it's going to be your last chance.'

Some days later, Wendover returned from an evening call in the village to find the bungalow empty and silent.

He had been to visit a case of skin cancer in its early stages, a four-year-old child. The women of the village knew he could do nothing, but they continued to call him out when the symptoms appeared, displaying a desperate faith. Occasionally, he was able to treat the accompanying attack of mild sickness; more often, he found both child and parent hysterical – the child sensing, perhaps, the massive damage to its future as a TV compère or fashion model – and could then do little more than offer sedatives. Suicide was not uncommon in adult cases. He found it considerably easier to fill out a death certificate than to lie about impending cures.

He had taken to walking on these visits: there was no urgency, and his experiences on the flyover had left him mistrustful of the roads. He dawdled home in the darkness, stopping to gaze over the bridge at the disturbed surface of the river, his tired brain populated with recollections of a dozen cottages:

Under a forty-watt lamp, the doughy face of the mother, her eyes flickering from the child to the forty-inch television; the father withdrawn, ashamed, offering him gassy bottled beer. They found it difficult to relate. They turned the volume down when he arrived. Colourful silent images mocked the sense of failure in the room as he shook his head over the child's marred complexion.

The bungalow was in a mess. In the bedroom,

drawers gaped open like slotted mechanical mouths; a pink under-slip lay in a frozen puddle on the dove-grey carpet; spilt face powder dusted the dressing table. The only bottles left were empty, their pastel labels displaying vacant promises. He stood for a moment, toying with the detritus on the table, tracing aimless designs with his forefinger in the spilt powder and analysing his reactions.

He found himself almost relieved: it had happened without the mess he'd expected. He felt nothing much in the way of regret. An appreciation of the silence. A vague incompleteness. He went wearily into his study and wrote answers to three offers for the practice – two from colleagues who, deluded by the reports of the cancer-research teams, saw a comfortable future in the half-completed overspill project, a lifetime of births, illnesses and deaths.

They were on Vanessa's territory. Though Wendover subscribed to none of the popular rumours – that the biochemists had an effective serum they were hanging ghoulishly on to (for the vaguest of reasons); that the entire research effort was in fact a front for a massive programme of chromosome manipulation (a project operated from the state gynaecological clinics and aimed at producing a first-generation, true-breeding mutation capable of handling huge doses of radiation); that they had in fact *caused* the outbreak and were shepherding it through its course (for further non-specific reasons) – he expected nothing. It was a galvanic kick. The frog was cold.

Presently, the silence began to annoy him. He got up and ranged about the bleak rooms, stopping only when he realized that he had been looking for a note or a letter, some final statement on Vanessa's part. There was nothing. A small, renegade element of regret insinuated itself into his skull. He was hungry, but the numbness was beginning to wear off, leaving him exposed and hurt, ill-equipped to deal with ordinary events and intrusions.

The door chimes sounded. Beyond the frosted glass of the front door, he made out a tall, bulky figure shifting uneasily from one foot to the other in the bright wash of light from the porch lamp. Not Vanessa, then. (Under the circumstances, the thought was illogical: Vanessa had too fine a sense of the dramatic to spoil her gesture by returning too soon, if at all. A letter, perhaps, if she regretted the move, or a telephone call; the tentative manoeuvres of reconciliation.)

A wave of cold eddied into the hall, inundating him. The man on the doorstep wore the yellow helmet of the Clearance Corps. Behind him, the stars were harsh points of light above the water pastures. He was slapping his hands together and whistling thinly. His breath steamed.

'There's been an accident,' he said.

The cold had set his face into a stereotype of condolence. He shuffled, sniffed, and wiped the sleeve of his donkey jacket under his nose.

Whatever the anaesthetic that dulled Wendover's nerves, it had been a short-term measure: he felt it desert him, leaving his brain peeled and raw, opening him to the chill of the real reality. Ersatz sympathy in the eyes of the Clearance man. He did it every day, and was probably trying hard. An unbelievable clarity of perception showed him every line of the man's face, interpreted every moment of his head. Grief welled in. He juggled images of destruction: the flesh boiling off the bones, streamers of burning turbine fuel, torn metal exploding away into the night. Suicide-prones should be prevented from holding licences. You'd better have me. He saw her limbs scattered and her head torn down to the bone structure. He didn't see anything.

The word 'accident' is a euphemism. What cold phrases.

He looked at the Clearance man and said very carefully: 'I know.'

The man gaped. He brushed past him and went into the cold night without a coat.

Leaning over the parapet of the flyover,

watching the deadly cars hum past in the gravel-eyed hours of the early morning, he felt guilt written on the inside of his head like the crabbed, illegible scrawl on a death certificate.

At that time the motorway stretched away into the future.

1: The Rabbit Snare

Some time later, slowly and clumsily, his hands unlocked. He stripped off the various husks of illusion; admitted to himself that thirty bare, sickening years had left their stigmata on both his mind and his world: and forced himself to face the ineluctable present . . .

Clement St John Wendover – sometime doctor and sophisticate of a derelict era – stood on the projecting arm of a smashed flyover eyeing hopelessly the ruin spread below him. His raw and toothless gums ached bitterly. The wind cut at him with spite and insistence.

He was not quite an old man. The eyes sunk deep in his bony, ulcerated face still radiated a certain youth of spirit. The stoop of his shoulders beneath the filthy gabardine was not the mark of age, but evidence of an insuperable weariness. And he was not frail: his thin body had acquired in three decades of scavenging a

distinct leathery fitness. There were calluses on
his palms and on his personality.

Vanessa haunted him only rarely now. Driven
from his waking mind by the urgencies of his
environment, she confined her brief appearances
to his dreams, where her face hovered over him
in the grasp of some indefinable passion: the
skin smooth, the eyes half-closed.

He would clutch at her, feeling heat in his old
cold groin, and her face would bleed, the beautiful skin breaking out in ulcers or peeling back
like the rind of an orange to reveal the perfectly
white skeleton, the inner grin. And he would
shudder awake to find refuge from the vision in
the comfortable dirt that surrounded him; in the
smell of his own body and the pain of his jaws.
Sometimes he awoke to find himself muttering
things, endearments. All day he might remember those, rolling them round his mouth. But by
the next day they would be gone, and even the
memory of them gone.

He was mourning the death of the road in
much the same fashion as he had mourned the
deaths the road itself had caused in cobalt dawns
a generation before.

A bleak desolation returned his stare. Thirty
winters had split the surface of the road, crazing
it like sunbaked mud. Clumps of grass thrusting
up from the cracks had turned it into an overgrown jigsaw. Here and there, hollyhocks had

taken root. A young elm sprouted from the central reservation. All the vegetation was pale, stunted, cancerous. But powerful, thought Wendover, to wreak such havoc in so short a time.

The fence hung in corroded festoons from its slim, phallic supports; like a fisherman's net hung out to dry. As far as he could see, none of the pillars had been disturbed; they marched, two files line astern, to the limits of vision, each one trailing its tattered spider web. Nightmare brides in iron veils.

Most of the flyovers in that vicinity were still intact, but Wendover's vantage point had been mined by an isolated Trotskyist demolition party during the internecine war that had led to subregional government. Huge lengths of ferroconcrete laced and linked with bent steel blocked the freeway.

Tumbled among the weeds were heaps of ochre rubbish and brittle rubber – the rusty, flaking wrecks of heavy turbo transport and private cars: underwriting the collapse of a social system that might as well have been a dream.

Even now his mind showed signs of refusing to face the truth. He was a guest who'd stayed too late; he was unwelcome. He caught himself sliding again into the bitter luxury of reverie, and, to prevent another lapse into the past, forced himself to leave the flyover. He was afraid that his growing recourse to the opiate of memory heralded the short, swift decline into senility and death. He did not want to die in this world.

He picked a careful way down to the old access road, skating on a talus of broken concrete and corroded steelwork, and went to inspect his snares. Despite the pain in his mouth, he could not keep from salivating at the thought of food. He wondered vaguely if now was the time to join the Tinhouse community: now, before he grew too old to forage for himself. They might be glad of a doctor, and his last two rabbits had been diseased and foul.

On the other hand, he avoided them churlishly in the past. And freedom was his sole real possession.

There was a small doe hare kicking feebly in one of the snares, its trapped rear leg cut to the bone. Its skin was as ulcerated as his own. Pelt fell away in lumps as he disengaged the leg from the loop of single-strand wire. The wire had once been the B-string of a Gibson Les Paul – he had burnt the guitar during a bad winter two years before. He had never tried to play it. The hare stared up at him from cataract-filmed brown eyes, unmoving. He discerned a mute plea in its eyes: whether for life or death, he didn't know.

He broke its neck anyway, and avoided the eyes thereafter. Carrying the animal by its ears,

he collected the rest of the snares – all empty –
and walked a mile to the bank of the canal.

The black, brackish water stank. Seventy
years uninterrupted mining by small aquatic
rodents had made the towpath an undefined
quagmire, prone to collapse in great chunks into
the water. The canal had been abandoned long
before the disaster. Etiolated sedge and bullrush
choked the waterway, and rotting, twisted hawthorn hemmed it in. Wendover lived in a Nissen
hut a few yards away from a silted-up lock
system; a deep, foreboding channel little more
than five feet wide, full of charcoal-grey mud.

Its odour ensured his privacy: the villagers
had a superstitious fear of bad smells, associat-
ing them, perhaps, with the memory of the
stinking cities during the period of plagues following the civil war; some of them believed that
as a doctor he was miraculously exempt from
the fevers of the canal area. They left him alone.
He already had something of the sacrosanct air
of the tribal shaman.

The interior of the hut was hot and incredibly
disordered. Five hundred or so square feet of
cement floor contained his collapsing bed; an
ancient, omnivorous black stove; and his
collection.

Gathering dust, a cross-section of a Saran-
wrapped age: a polaroid camera; twenty-seven
capsules of Penicillin V in a plastic phial; a

photograph of an oiled-up seagull; a colour television; a 1/96th scale polystyrene replica of an Apollo control module; a *matraque*; a mildewed pile of dirty magazines; a photograph of J. G. Ballard; a rolled-up poster advertising vaginal deodorant; a fruit machine; a morocco-bound edition of *The Stud Book*, a photograph of Che Guevara, signed; an oral contraceptive wallet; an 800-watt amplifier. A junkshop desolation of broken furniture, dusty books, and electrical equipment that would never operate again.

Wendover considered it sourly. He had begun the collection years ago, motivated by a caretaker impulse that he did not understand. It continued to grow, almost of its own volition.

Sometimes he savoured the fine irony of it: thirty years ago he had believed himself liberated; now he lived in a stupor of nostalgia.

He flung the snares down among the other rubbish, squatted awkwardly down by the stove, and began to skin the hare. He muttered to himself. His gums ached.

He had been trying for half an hour to eat the animal when someone hammered on the door.

He gave up the unequal struggle at once, glad of an excuse to stop chewing and relieve the agony of his loose teeth. He took the big Smith & Wesson from its biscuit tin beneath the lousy bed. The racket grew louder as he slipped the weapon into his overcoat pocket. Keeping one hand on it, he opened the door a few inches and peered out.

Immediately, the handle was wrenched away from him.

The door flew open, bruising his collar bone, and sent him staggering backwards, his gun arm numbed. He caught his heel in the trailing flex of a two-kilowatt electric fire and sprawled among the rest of the useless paraphernalia. A fingernail of pain scraped delicately at the base of his spine. The foresight of the pistol had snagged the lining of his pocket. He pulled at it feverishly. Lying there, his brain refusing to function at survival pitch, he realized that for all practical purposes he was as redundant as the surrounding junk: he was old.

A red mist obscured his vision. Fear squeezed him under the heart. And then he began to cry out, because there was some sort of beast slavering at his throat.

Abandoning the pistol, he tried to keep it off with his hands. His fingers hooked into ruffs of matted hair. The thing's breath was warm and foetid. He flailed helplessly at the muzzle. He passed out.

When he woke up he was lying in bed, sweating. Someone was kneeling in front of the stove, gazing into its open belly, fondling a huge muddy wolfhound. Wendover twitched at the recollection of its teeth at his jugular vein.

Hearing the movement, the intruder got to his feet and looked down at him.

He was tall and thin, dressed in tight, patched jeans and a dark reefer jacket with incongruous chrome buttons. His wiry blond hair was brushed straight back from his forehead and ears, falling in waves clear to his shoulders; the result being to throw his face into a birdlike and predatory prominence. An aquiline nose completed the resemblance. His large eyes were grey and as amused as the slight twist of his full lips. He stepped forward, offering the pan Wendover had used for cooking the hare. His right leg was bent awkwardly at the knee, his gait stiff.

His name was Harper, and he was a second-generation Tinhouser. Wendover, who had misset the crippled leg fifteen years before when Harper was eleven years old, regarded him biliously and ignored the slightly ironical gesture. He looked with suspicion at the dog, which was sitting quietly by the stove, apparently fascinated by the flames.

Harper withdrew the pan, set it back on the stove. Smelling the hare, the wolfhound whined. It slavered a little, hanging out its tongue. Harper growled at it affectionately and ruffled its hackles, picking something up from the floor with his free hand. When he turned back to Wendover he was still smiling. A length of damp rope, brown and rotted, hung from his fingers. It was newly frayed at one end. He swung it gently and said: 'I'm sorry, Doctor. It really was an accident. The rope broke.' His voice was low and gentle.

'Pah,' said Wendover.

Abruptly, Harper stopped smiling. His attention seemed to wander. He studied the simmering pan.

'You can't eat it, can you? Life could be easier . . .' he swung round, his eyes intense. 'Life could be easier for you.'

Wendover shrugged. Their relationship was ambivalent, often unstable. The sympathy might switch at any moment to anger or contempt.

'I'm not ready for the village, if that's what you mean. Give it to the dog, I'm not ready for that, there's something here I value.'

Harper laughed, a short bark that might have come from the dog. His visits to the doctor had become rarer since both of them had given up hope over the twisted leg. His lips writhed briefly over white teeth.

'Freedom, is it, Doctor?'

Wendover swung his legs over the edge of the bed. Nausea welled up as he came vertical. The dog fixed him with blue-brown depthless eyes and growled. He took the pan, placed it on the floor. The animal rose, still growling.

'He won't take it from you, Doctor.'

Harper stood in front of the pan, made encouraging noises in the back of his throat. The wolfhound walked forward. One foreleg was deformed so that its head dipped every time the limb came down. Harper said nothing, just grinned at Wendover, watching his face. He sat down next to his familiar. Then he said. 'I call him Vulcan.' Wendover kept his mouth shut. After a while, Harper looked away.

'Why are you here?' Wendover began to pull absently on a loose thread at his cuff. 'What does Tinhouse want from me? You didn't make the trip just to show me your pet.'

'We have a problem. For you, a professional problem.'

'You need a medicine-man?'

'Oh, fuck off . . .' His lips straightened and his jaw muscles stood out tight. He really was very young.

There was a pause, punctuated by the wolfhound's feverish grunts as it nosed the pan round the floor in an attempt to get at the juice coagulated in its corners. Harper drew his knees up to his chin, wrapped his arms round them, and spoke into the fire.

'There's been a birth. It would be better if you came now.'

He got up without looking at the doctor and limped to the door. The dog left its task immediately, looked up to snarl at Wendover, and followed, head nodding.

Wendover slid his hand into the pocket of the gabardine, feeling for the pistol. It was still there. He searched among the rubbish, pulled out the ragged duffel-bag that contained his ludicrous medical kit. Harper watched from the door, eyes flickering over the shambles. 'You know, Doctor,' he said, 'you might set up a business with that lot. It's quite a promising collection.'

Outside, the wind bit their ears; sent the dog running in circles; fluffed the surface of the canal into a network of ripples. It hissed bleakly through the thorn and rattled a loose inspection plate on the battered engine cowling of the turbine car that stood ten yards away at the end of the dirt track. It was a big, pathetic vehicle, lost and out of context. Rust stains raked the full length of one side like the clawmarks of a steel beast. Its scarlet cellulose was blistered, its chromium leer knocked crooked, shabby as the make-up of an old, raddled tart. And waiting for two tramps, thought Wendover. Which is some bring-down.

Hunched up against the wind, yelling occasionally at his dog, Harper trudged over to the short, thick-set young boy who was leaning against the driver's door, whistling tunelessly into the wind and nodding his large, doll-like head.

They punched each other about by way of

greeting, the wolfhound leaping around them in mock ferocity, yelping histrionically. The commotion died away as Wendover approached. Harper, breathing heavily, his face red, said: 'Doctor, this is Arm.' There was a quaint touch of formality to his voice. The child stepped forward and offered his hand.

It was big and spade-shaped and grizzled with black hair. His left arm hung, crooked at the elbow, from a muscled adult's torso; the fingertips brushed his knee. His legs – gaudy in cut down op-art slacks – might have belonged to a five-year-old child, had they not been warped and buckled after forty-odd years supporting the body above the tiny pelvis. Ancient eyes the colour of old cement brooded at Wendover from under a single heavy eyebrow.

Unnerved, Wendover hesitated, looking stupidly at the extended hand.

'Sod off, then, if you feel like that,' said the dwarf equably. His voice was a thick catarrhal rumble.

Wendover shook the hand, which was blacknailed, scarred, and immensely hard, and muttered, 'I'm sorry, I . . . '

'Forget it. Your face don't look too good either.' His mouth split grotesquely, revealing broken down teeth. He wheezed. His shoulders shook.

'He likes you,' said Harper.

Someone had knocked out the driving seat of

the turbo and set a low box over the sheared mounting lugs. The pedals were blocked up with sections of two by four so that the dwarf could reach them. Harper sat crammed in the back. The dog dribbled on him. In the confined space it smelt. Arm spun the rear wheels needlessly and dragged it hard up the track in a welter of mud and noise.

'What's the radiation count like?' Wendover asked Harper, without much hope that anything had changed.

Harper shrugged.

'It was level six months back,' he said, 'but we haven't taken any readings since. Arnold Plewes dropped the Geiger. Pauce shot him on the spot. There aren't any spares.'

Out on the clearway, the wind plucked and tore at the car. Arm chuckled and accelerated. Wendover watched the lurching horizon like a rabbit watching a ferret.

2: The House of Holloway Pauce

Tinhouse straggled in a ragged curve half in and half out of a fair-sized lunate covert of scruffy birches, a dismal ersatz village constructed mainly of galvanized metal set on timber frames. Some of the community who had no access to the standard materials had built shacks using sheets of asbestos vandalized from the deserted overspill projects. A minority had taken tin cans or old car bodies, beaten them flat, and lashed them together to form crude wall sections. They had built close to the wood to take advantage of its skimpy protection against the prevailing wind; but now the wind-break was leafless, and Tinhouse was chilled to its wooden bones. In the wind the whole place set up an eldritch rattle, like the playing of a giant tambourine.

Out of the three-acre wilderness rose the house of Holloway Pauce, a late-Victorian red brick farmhouse and its ancillary buildings arranged round three sides of a square. A veinous tracery of dead ivy crawled over it, lending a flayed appearance to its pink-brown walls. There were no weeds growing between the cobbles of the square, but the moss-encrusted dormers sagged wearily.

Turbine alternately racing and groaning, the car slid and yawed its way across the poached ground between the shacks. Ragged children dabbled in the morass that surrounded each one. Wendover, staring numbly through the mud-streaked windscreen at an incoherent montage of small crippled and cancered limbs, thin as chicken shanks, reflected that nothing had changed in ten years: the place still infected him with a cold, enveloping depression; he felt an intense empathy with the children, destructive and frustrating because of his utter medical impotence. His brain iced up after the first few yards of Tinhouse proper; he experienced simultaneously a sick fascination and a desire to avert his eyes and never look again: he felt like some incredibly perverted voyeur, a second, objective Genet, developing his religion of degradation. The outbuildings of the farm loomed up and he thankfully turned his eyes on them. The brickwork was crumbling.

'Pauce'll be in the shack with the woman,' said Harper, 'but we'll have to leave the wagon in the yard or it'll never move again.'

It began to rain as they clambered out, a
sudden squall blustering from beyond the
birches and setting the village clattering and
roaring insistently. Each lean-to acted as an
amplifier, boosting the muted hiss of water on
metal until the tambourine was replaced by an
immense unbalanced engine.

There was an armoured car parked in the
courtyard. An early-model Tuppen, the marque
current a decade before the increase in radiation, it bulked massively up from sixty-inch
heavy-duty tyres, its canted steel sides filthy
with rust and caked with black loam. Grey
daubs like leprous infections on its olive-drab
flanks showed where its insignia had been
painted out: it had probably changed hands a
dozen times during the breakdown of national
administration, and half a dozen since. The
barrels of twin 50mm pneumatic cannon poked
out of its turret. Wendover had not seen it
before, and it worried him.

Sporadic raiding still occurred between the
regions, and within them on a village-to-village
basis: Pauce might have obtained the thing as
an insurance policy. But, on the other hand, if
he had decided that the Geiger counter (they
were still fetish objects in the majority of com-
munities, even though there had been no signifi-
cant change in the level of radioactivity since
the initial surges of the disaster period) must be

replaced by whatever means came to hand, including piracy, then the end of Tinhouse was in sight. None of the militant villages existed as such for long; there was a continuous process of attack and induction, combination and recombination, that destroyed autonomy. Pauce, if he got on the ambition circuit, stood as much chance of ending up a serf as he did the ruler of a principality.

Harper nodded at the machine, his lips curling.

'How do you like the status symbol? Didn't they use to use gun-carriages as biers for dead kings?'

His face contracted, seeming to hood itself. Wendover guessed that all was not well with Harper and Pauce.

'Does it work?' he countered, not wishing to make a statement that placed him in either camp.

The cripple sensed it. He made a small moue of self-effacement. Then he grimaced in a melodramatic parody of conspiracy, his features moving a further step towards the aquiline.

'Hush,' he said, 'or you'll offend Arm. He lives for that bloody old thing.'

Arm just grinned. He fell behind them as they waded through the mud and the thunder of the rain. His ungainly shuffle was quite fast enough for him to keep up, but he had gathered a following of sickly children who chattered a mass of queries about the state of the Tuppen – how fast, and would it really shoot, no, *really*. Wendover found the noise irritating, but Arm responded with the grotesque grin chopping his face in two – a pied piper from long-done mobile battles and clearways packed with wailing turbos. The wolfhound held itself aloof from the children, growling if they came too close. None of them tried to pet it.

Harper stopped outside a degenerating hovel, the basic constructional unit of which was the ten-gallon JP4 drum, hammered into a crude panel and coated with umber cellulose primer in a vain attempt to prevent corrosion. Some nine panels had gone into the fascia, riveted loosely together. From inside came the cold cry of a hungry baby, punctuated by the creak of the warped plyboard door. A crowd of thin, sunken-cheeked Tinhousers had gathered in front of it, fidgeting and staring blankly about.

They fell back as the cripple led Wendover to the door. He recognized some of them from his last visit. He put his hand to the latch. It was covered immediately by Harper's lean fingers, which prevented him gently from working it.

'Before we go in,' he murmured, his lips close to Wendover's ear, 'I don't want you to be surprised by anything Pauce says or does, because . . .'

Wendover removed the restraining hand, certain now that Harper's reasons for wanting him here differed a good deal from those of Pauce.

'Keep me out of this,' he warned.

The place was dingy and littered, pervaded by a crepuscular light which barely changed in intensity as the daylight filtered in. Although the draughts hissing through the cracked walls assured a constant cross-current of fresh air, it smelt strongly of stale lives, the peculiar reek that epitomised Tinhouse, compounded of sweat, dirt, no point and no hope; the stink of people who have been too long in the crisis of poverty to care. Wendover, his eyes slow in adjusting to the gloom, hesitated on the threshold. He could detect only unreal shapes.

His vision cleared. At the far end of the single room, a woman whose white, washed-out face seemed to luminesce with pain lay supine on a flock mattress (this grey-striped and bursting, the innards hanging suggestively out of it). A single threadbare blanket, once brightly coloured, was drawn up as far as her shoulders. She was shivering, and crooning in a low voice to the child that presumably lay beside her. Of this, Wendover could make out only a small dark object emerging from the lips of the blanket.

As his eyes grew accustomed to the light, he

discerned several lice scurrying over the mattress. Whatever the pain, the woman's eyes were fired with it, big blue fires in the drained bony face. The rat's tails of hair about her thin neck and shoulders were yellow-grey. She did not look at him as he entered: her eyes were fixed on the man who was leaning against the wall at the foot of the pallet.

Holloway Pauce wore a gold lamé suit.

He took his ease, and the unbelievable clothes hung off his spare, scarecrow frame like the cerements of a dead emperor. He was fully six foot eight tall, his huge head, with its nimbus of silky auburn hair, over-topping Wendover by a good ten inches. His knobby limbs protruded from the cuffs of jacket and trousers, spindly and entomic. He wore grey suède cowboy boots, cut high, and his mild, preoccupied eyes peered from behind round, steel-rimmed spectacles. The skin cancers on his face were covered by a layer of pancake make-up, turning his prominent features into a yellow mask.

He looked theatrical and more than faintly ridiculous, but as he swung his massive head with slow, ursine deliberation toward Wendover – revealing that the mask had cracked, leaving deep, scar-like fissures in his cheeks – the doctor sensed behind those silly, benign eyes something cold and unpleasant. In motion, his body was contained and powerful.

A young man would have merely appeared bizarre in the golden drag: Holloway Ableson Pauce was sixty years old, and he radiated the intense mythopoeic quality of a harlequin. The suit glittered faintly in the gloom, like the skin of a merman.

'Ah, Wendover,' he said, absently. 'I hope you're well?'

The obsolete courtesy should have sounded absurd. His voice was sharp, his syllables precisely articulated. But he wasn't there: he cared so little, he might have been years removed from his own voice.

'Hello, Pauce. What's the matter?'

'Hasty as ever, Wendover. Am I keeping you from some other business?' He smiled colourlessly, then continued, 'I want you to examine the child . . .'

Wendover unslung the duffel-bag without waiting for him to finish, and walked over to the pallet. The woman turned her lambent eyes on him like a half-wild animal, her arm slipping round the tiny mound under the blanket. The reflex gesture of maternity. He tried to smile at her, but found the muscles of his mouth too stiff and unpractised. Instead, he asked: 'How do you feel? Was it difficult?' Pauce's voice cut in on him from the shadows.

'Forget the woman, Doctor. The woman is not our main concern.'

Wendover faced him. The long golden jacket had fallen open, revealing that the wide belt slung round the man's hips supported an oiled leather holster, fastened with a brass stud. Harper and the dwarf had come in and were standing by the door. Harper was grinning.

'I don't live here, Pauce,' said Wendover slowly, 'and I owe you nothing. Don't forget that.'

Pauce's mask became expressionless.

Wendover turned back the blanket. Still obsessed with Pauce, the woman made an abortive grab at her child, then seemed to contract and withdraw.

Somewhere else in the world, Pauce said, 'Arm, the vehicle is quite ready, then?'

The child lay huddled compactly against her swollen left breast. It was a mutant, but of a kind he had never seen before. Dry leathery skin covered its body like a suit of mail, creased and loose over its joints. It was mottled and scaly.

Initially, he thought it was a normal baby that had been born completely cancered or scabbed; but when he felt the skin, pinching a little of it over the tiny ribcage, he found it hard and thick, its texture uniform and tough. Once again, he thought of armour – this time not chain-mail, but the carapace of an armadillo, the chitin of an insect. Its mouth was open on a long, flexible tongue that quivered faintly. It was panting, which suggested that the strange skin might not sweat. It waved its limbs slowly in the diminishing pocket of warm air above its mother's body, the stiff integument flexing at knees and elbows. He covered it as it began to drown in some afterbirth sea of sorrow and managed a wan smile of encouragement for the mother. He turned to Pauce, trying to formulate words that would convey exactly the half-glimpsed memory that had flashed like brief neon at the periphery of his brain.

'Is it normal, Wendover?'

'Normal? I don't quite see your point. None of us are that any more. What we have here is something that hasn't happened before . . .'

Pauce made an impatient downward motion of his hand. Before he could speak, Harper intervened, some inner strain distorting his features.

'Oh but it *has*, Doctor! Ask him. Ask Pauce what . . .' He stopped as Pauce swung round on him, his old body moving with an unexpected fluid grace. A heavy-calibre automatic pistol had blossomed at the end of his arm like a steel flower.

'Shut up,' he said quietly.

He turned back to Wendover, shifting his position so he could cover Harper at the same time. 'Is it normal, Doctor?' he repeated.

Wendover tried to ignore the gun. 'Strictly,

no,' he admitted, 'but you didn't need me to tell you that. You have eyes . . .'

Pauce seemed to relax. The mask betrayed nothing, but the tenseness went out of his limbs. Then he levelled the pistol at Wendover and said: 'Move away, Doctor. I can't allow divergance on this scale. Move out of the way.'

'You wanted an opinion, Pauce. That hide is a radiation shield. There were rumours. I wouldn't have believed it could be done.'

'Don't talk rubbish. Move away, Wendover.'

At that point, Wendover committed himself. Until then he had watched the decline of the world with passive acceptance; taken refuge in dreams because he could not bear the present. His memories had not been the stigmata of senility but those of retreat. Because the child represented somebody's future, he became involved with the present.

He shot Pauce without taking the pistol out of his raincoat pocket.

He saw the bullet connect, ripping into the fleshy part of the man's thigh and knocking him back against the wall. Pauce grunted. His automatic described a glittering arc and landed at Wendover's feet. The woman on the bed began to scream. Short, tearing cries in the vacuum following the roar of the shot. There was blood on the lamé as Pauce slid slowly down the wall; and blood also on the metal behind him, sprayed

from the exit-hole of the bullet. The crowd outside hummed with a single satisfied voice – they
had come to hear an execution. Pauce was trying
to say something, but he couldn't stop groaning.
Cordite smoke stung Wendover's eyes, feather-
ing up from the holed fabric of his coat. He
wanted to vomit.

Harper lurched forward. He pressed his face
up to the doctor's, dissolving, breaking up with
emotion; thrust so close and jerking dementedly,
it was a gargantuan Guignol.

'What the bloody hell d'you think you're doing,
Wendover? What the bloody . . .'

Wendover thrust him away.

'Isn't that what you wanted?' he shouted, glad
of the relief: 'Isn't that why you brought me
here? The False King deposed? The Revolution?
Something *you* hadn't the stomach for?'

Harper's face stopped twitching. He was shaking. He listened to Wendover with an expression
of disbelief. He said, 'Oh God. No, Doctor. That
wasn't it. That wasn't it at all.' His face threatened to crumble again. He appeared to be
arranging his next words. 'Listen,' he said.
'Those kids. Pauce killed three of them. In
public. I hoped you might change his mind, I
persuaded him to get your word on this one, I
hoped you might . . . Not kill him, not . . . I don't
know anything about this radiation thing.'

'He's not dead. Use your eyes,' said Wendover,

reflecting that he and the cripple had switched roles somewhat: 'It's a clean hole, it went right through. It'll heal.'

The dwarf, who had come up and was bending over the injured man, nodded an agreement. He said: 'What will you do now?'

'Attempt to get out without being torn apart by that lot.' Wendover indicated the mob beyond the door, feeling his new assurance ebb rapidly. Something touched the skirt of his coat.

He looked down at the woman, who had stopped screaming. She was offering him the child. There were funnels of tear erosion in the grime on her face. Divining her intention, Clement Wendover, the committed man, took it from her. Christ, he thought. Oh Christ. She stared up at the baby for some seconds, then turned wearily to face the wall.

'I'll look after it,' he told the back of her neck, 'I'll . . .' But he couldn't think of anything more to say. He felt that he had made a fool of himself. He walked to the door; found Harper and Arm behind him; said, 'Well?'

Harper had regained control. A suspicion of his cocky smile flickered at the corners of his mouth. His face was still pale. 'Welcome back, Doctor,' he said. Then: 'You'll need help with that.'

'Back?'

'Back to the land of the living. I thought you'd never make it.'

The crowd fell back at first, until they missed Pauce and saw the guns and the child. Then they surged in, surly, but still passive. They didn't quite understand.

Holloway Pauce lurched out of the hut, a bloody gold spectre clinging to the door and mouthing painfully. The situation fulminated. A big fellow laid his hands on Arm, who had no weapon. The dwarf swung a horny fist into his face, felling him. The wolfhound began to yelp and growl. Somebody swiped at it, and it tore his hand. Wendover ran, the press parting under the threat of the revolver. Arthritic hands snatched for the child, and he pistol-whipped a white, shouting face. He wasn't amazed by himself. Harper fired a shot into the air to break up the *mêlée* centred on the heaving body of the dwarf. It was a mistake.

Three sharp reports came from somewhere in the mob. The wolfhound howled, danced frenziedly, guttered into silence. Harper bellowed. Pauce's automatic jumped in his hand. He shot three of them, and his features were distorted once more.

They broke away, bullets thumping wetly into the mud that hampered their feet. Harper twisted often in mid-stride to return the fire; but Wendover, crushing the child to his side, felt a searing pain in his lungs as the unaccustomed effort began to tell on him, making use of the pistol difficult. His feet slithered about on the greasy surface of the courtyard. The shots were louder here, echoing back from the blind buildings.

They made it to the armoured car, when Wendover and the cripple stood holding off the avant-couriers of the crowd while Arm undogged the hatch.

As they climbed in, the flat heavy concussion of the pneumatics turned its hull into a vibrating drum. The dwarf blanketed the yard with pyrotic shells that burst against the red brick walls in brief white sparks of light. It was not necessary to fire into the crowd; immediately the blind, black-snouted turret began to turn, they ran. Stray shells fired one or two of the hovels beyond the square. They burned unenthusiastically.

Harper dropped into the driving compartment. The turbine coughed and caught, and then they were barreling behind Holloway Pauce's house, crashing through the birches in a mist of steam as the down-draught exhaust boiled the water from the mud beneath them.

3: The Real-life Romances

Morag came up from the south, from a fishing village on the eastern seaboard where gulls like dirty scraps of cloth clustered on the corroded skeletons of off-shore oil rigs.

She travelled by night and on foot, following the cracked moonlit perspectives of the old motorways, avoiding the derelict cities because they were haunted. She slept in wrecked cars and stole small amounts of food from shabby hamlets along the way. She was ten months pregnant, so long she had given up expecting the child, which was her second. Occasionally she was troubled by contractions and pains, but they were sterile: it was almost as if the child suspected life outside her for what it was, a cruelty. She talked to it, but nothing would tempt it out.

Come out.

Too cold, and nowhere to go.

Come out and I'll warm you.

No need to move here, nothing is moving here.

There had been times, before she left the fishing commune, when she mourned the loss of her thin, still-youthful body. This partial decline of youth had spurred her departure: gazing out over the grey, silted estuary during the evening following the death of her first child, she had felt her depression mingled with the air of desolation surrounding the scuttled hulks of coastal hovercraft, creating a powerful but undefined dissatisfaction. Now, shapeless and heavy, with nothing solved by the aimless journey north, she had grown used to her own clumsiness and forgotten her reasons for quitting the village. She was twenty years old.

It was her stealing that finally brought the child out: she stole some bread one night and they found her the next morning.

She was sleeping under some gorse, in a tunnel between the thick, fibrous stems, olive green foliage above her. Asleep, her head was packed with the gorse, and something was pursuing her through it without making any noise: she had a hollow sense of foreboding, but could hear only her own footsteps. She woke suddenly to find herself staring into a glaring patch of light with ragged edges, across which shifted pale swift clouds. It framed a child's face, which loomed over her, brown and wizened. Its hands, thin and scabby, had pulled the gorse apart. Its legs were in the tunnel, almost touching her prostrate body. It was looking down at her with detached interest. 'Hello,' she said.

The child opened its eyes very wide, then turned and stumbled off quickly through the bushes. It had seen the half-loaf beside her. The foliage sprang back into place, occluding the sky and rustling softly, and she was left alone in the tunnel. She knew she should get up and go; the child had seen the loaf; children remembered because they never got enough to eat. She was asleep again when they came for her.

Two women with thick-boned, concave faces and cropped, matted hair quartered the gorse patch, shouting to one another. Morag woke, tensed, but saw no point in trying to run. Her belly slowed her down. They were ugly. One of them had warts all over her face, big, cracked excrescences; the other had hair growing in thick black tufts from her cheekbones. They were dressed in voluminous skirts which they held out of reach of the gorse spines with large, red-knuckled hands.

Morag tried to crawl away along the tunnel, and they found her. The warty one dragged her upright and spat in her face, her long upper lip curling back like a horse's, her eyes empty.

Morag shrieked and bit, horrified by the eyes. The other one knocked her down.

'You pregnant little bastard,' she said, grinning.

They dragged her to the village and stood her in the middle of a pocked crumbling road between faded cottages. There was a smell of sewage.

Women surrounded her, spilling from the cottages, laughing and hawking and spitting. Here and there she glimpsed a flash of colour, a scarf, a shawl. She was tired and hungry and the smell made her sick. There were no men, but the women were tall and bony, with similar scooped-out faces and stringy, powerful limbs. Some of them displayed defects: three breasts; seven fingers, the extra two being webbed with rubbery skin.

Two of them struggled noisily for a length of knotted nylon rope.

They beat her, those not participating pressing forward to see better. There was excitement in the air. Just before the child began to stir, Morag saw one of them fall down, shuddering and pawing at herself.

'Oh, oh, oh,' she moaned.

It took some time for the rope to break the skin of her back, but by then there was a slow agony in her belly and blood on her thighs, and she was down on the road, biting at the tarmac and screaming. Things went grey.

She lay waiting for the bleeding to stop, breathing slowly and carefully. She had had quite an easy time of it compared to the first. Every few minutes she tried to elicit some reaction from the baby. When she was stronger she hauled herself up on one elbow and looked along the length of her body at it. She fainted again. The child that had discovered her in the gorse came to look at her. It stayed for half an hour – disinterested eyes, thumb in mouth – and she was quite glad of its company. It wandered off suddenly, like an animal losing interest. She began to shiver. She cried out, but the village looked deserted, the women had gone; nothing moved behind their cottage doors, or if it did, it was very silent. The wind rose and wrapped her hair about her face. Someone answered her.

A man came out of the nearest cottage, moving jerkily, hopping and limping. He wore bright blue velvet trousers, a white shirt with lace ruffles, and a bottle-green jacket sewn with sequins in spiral patterns. There were heavy gold rings on his fingers, and his thin long mournful face was entirely without cancers, white and smooth. His shoulder length black hair was tied back with a brocade ribbon. He had a wispy little beard. His feet were bare but clean, and shackled to his raw, swollen left ankle was a yard length of shiny chain, joining him like an umbilical cord to the doorpost of the cottage. It clinked when he came on. He was quick and furtive, stopping every few strides to scan the empty street and paying particular attention to the windows of the buildings. He carried a bucket from which water slopped regularly, soaking one leg of his beautiful trousers. He hugged a bundle of clothes to his chest. The chain brought him up short five feet away from her.

'Fuck,' he said miserably. 'Oh damn and blast it . . .' He sat down, spilling more water.

'You'll have to come to me,' he said.

The water was warm. He had put salt in it, and it hurt her back. He detached her from the baby, then crawled off a couple of yards to be ill. He made her eat some food that had been wrapped up in the bundle. Finally, he dressed her, tearing off the bloody wreckage of her own clothes and getting her into denims, faded plaid shirt, a leather jacket with a heavy fleece lining. During this process he became increasingly agitated, glaring about and trembling nervously when the wind made noises across the roofs. Deep lines scored his face; his mouth turned down at the corners; he muttered unpleasantly.

Across the street a curtain moved.

'Oh fuck!' he gasped. He shuddered the whole length of his spine, turned, and leapt away, his chain rattling as he back-tracked it.

A wild screech rose over the moan of the wind. Abruptly, the street was full of women. Morag began to scuttle away crabwise, leaving the dead child, making for a lane that led into open country, pain scalding from her shoulder blades to her groin. But the women took no notice of her. They clustered round the chained man, their arms rising and falling rapidly. He wailed.

She was upset about the baby: after ten months she had wanted to get to know it a little better. The bleeding stopped. She was forced to take off her shirt several times when it stuck to her back. It became stiff, but that added nothing to the discomfort. The pain stayed with her for a week – at that time, she was not fond of herself, because of the vomiting – but after that it seemed to get better.

She found the motorway again, moved a short way along it, heading north instinctively, then stayed for two days in an abandoned car, listening to the wind and not moving much.

In the back seat of the car she found a book called *Real Life Romances*. Most of it was a soft block of pulp, lumps of yellow and blue mould growing on it, but the final page was intact:

True Love fascinated her. She read the words with difficulty, then learned them by heart. At night she recited them softly to herself, visualizing the lovers.

She started walking again at noon on the third day, and left the motorway when the fence supports began to resemble dream women in steel veils who said, If you hadn't stolen the bread, you would still have your baby.

She watched from the uncomfortable interior of a hawthorn thicket as the three men left the hut in the red car, then stood on the concrete lip of the choked lock, wrinkling her nose against the smell and wondering if there was anybody left behind. She was straight and almost youthful again – a denim dryad, slightly scruffy and contemplating thievery, her dirty blonde hair wild in the wind. After keeping still for ten minutes, she found her head beginning to swim unpleasantly. She was tired and cold. She walked quietly up to the hut and tried the door, ready to run. But it opened quite easily and the place was empty.

The collage of unrelated objects revealed as the door swung back was something of a magic garden. She wandered among the relics, breathing on glassy polyestered surfaces and watching the condensation form over the distorted image, entranced by the multiple reflections and chrome highlights. The *Stud Book* enthralled her, its interminable lists of meaningless names acquiring deep secondary interpretations by way of their very irrelevance to things and states of being she knew. She riffled persistently through it, her sense of time destroyed; but finally the open stove proved more of an attraction: she put the book carefully down and sat with the heat tightening the skin of her face. Soporific warmth drew her back from a desultory search for food.

It became obvious that she should leave, that there was nothing here but the chance of the men returning and finding her. As she drowsed, a sense of urgency welled up momentarily only to be swept away by a fantasy of True Love. She slept curled like a child on the hard cement floor.

The gigantic crane-fly with weird amber eyes flew through her dreams, diving and gyring as it blundered about looking for an exit; whining and breaking its grotesque dangling limbs against the walls of her skull. The soft touch of its wings was unbearable: she shifted and kicked in a miserable half-sleep. Then the insistent drone resolved itself into the sound of a turbine, very close, shaking the iron roof in sympathy as it raced up through its power curve and down again. She turned her face wearily to the door and lay still. There was nothing else to do.

The little old man came in first. He was flustered, red-faced under his patina of cancers, his bald, scarred scalp shining with perspiration. There was a hunted, narrow set to his veined blue eyes. He was saying (his face animated, his brown, rotting mouth flapping open like a string puppet's),

'It won't take long, Harper. Besides, Pauce isn't going anywhere on that leg.'

His voice was reedy but urgent, a petulant old voice raised to compete with both the turbine and the crying of the child in the crook of his elbow.

Pressed into the stiff, dirt-glazed cloth of his

coat, its arms and legs moving aimlessly and impotently, it heaved dryly between sobs. Despite its mould-coloured ulcerous skin, she felt an abrupt surge not of maternity but of fellow-feeling. It seemed very defenceless. She formed a link on the animal level: a shared position.

Harper, who was much younger, followed hard on the old man's heels, gesticulating. He was quite nice.

'What about the other turbo? He has that. And the villagers.'

'We need the stuff. There are fifty rounds here somewhere. They haven't got anything big enough to tackle us anyway. It would take a bomb to open that wagon. Stop worrying . . .'

'But that's my *point!* While we're here, we aren't *in* it!'

Because there was no sense in hiding, and because the baby reminded her of her own, Morag got to her feet as they came through the wilderness of primary colours and dusty chrome. She did it without any fuss.

Wendover brought himself up sharply, his mouth falling open and a spasm shaking his body. He fumbled his free hand into his coat pocket, crushing the child harder to him to prevent it from falling. His eyes were wide. He couldn't get his hand out of his pocket once it was in. Outside, the turbine reached a crescendo and stopped. The child followed it into silence, as if it were an organic extension of the engine.

Harper said, 'What . . . ?' He had a gun.

Morag tried to smile. She didn't want to be shot.

'I think your baby's hungry,' she said.

She went up to Wendover (he had stopped fumbling and was staring blankly from her to the child as though he were trying to register a connection) and touched his arm near the elbow.

'You'll hurt it, holding it so tight.'

He didn't relax. He didn't seem to hear. Harper limped up and thrust the gun into her ribs, just under her left breast. He too looked bemused.

'Don't shoot me,' she said, 'because I can feed it. I had one. The milk is still there . . .' She didn't know whether it was. She started to unfasten her shirt. When she came to the place where the gun barrel bit, she pushed it away without flinching. Then she held her arms out for the child, waiting for the gun to go off. Wendover hesitated, eyes searching her face, something else there besides puzzlement. Harper had lowered the gun slightly; but she was still conscious of it.

'Please,' she said.

He gave her the child. She took it gently, and sensing that the crisis had been reached and passed, turned away. Its skin was warm and dry against hers. She was all right with the feeding. Behind her, the silence continued for a moment. Harper broke it.

'For God's sake . . .'

Over her shoulder, she saw him regarding the pistol as if it had betrayed him. He grasped the old man's shoulder and shook it.

'You can't just . . . Who the hell is she?'

'I don't believe it matters,' answered Wendover. 'Presuming the child is capable of feeding from a normal woman – which, in the circumstances, I suppose it must be – then I think this solves a problem we hadn't even considered.' A faint smile touched his tired face. 'Are *you* in any condition to suckle a baby, Harper? Or Arm, possibly? I'm a bit old, myself . . .'

Harper opened his mouth, looking piqued. Then he laughed.

'I keep underestimating you,' he said.

Morag murmured things to the baby, only marginally aware of the talk. She had discovered a reason for her sense of loss. Wendover had to repeat his query twice before it registered.

'We're going away,' he said, raising one arm and motioning vaguely as if to indicate their line of travel. 'We must take the child. Perhaps you might come, take care of it?'

She hardly considered the question, merely nodded; the idea that they might take the child and leave her hadn't occurred to her. It had drifted off to sleep. She stroked its horny arms, her fingers dwelling lightly on the loose flesh of its joints. She'd seen them before, of course, but this one was different.

'Are you taking it back to the others?' she asked.

Wendover wrinkled his forehead. 'If you mean the village – ?'

'I don't know about villages,' she told him, surprised by his stupidity. 'But there's lots of them down south. They hide, but everybody knows.'

They hid all right. They had become very wary now: they were rarely caught when they stole fish from the estuary villages. She had never expected to be looking after one.

An incredulous expression crinkled the flesh at the corners of his eyes and mouth. He didn't believe her – or perhaps it was that he wanted to believe her and was trying hard not to. She couldn't tell. He was pretty old.

'More of them?' he pressed. 'You're sure?'

She nodded again. He turned jubilantly to Harper.

'You heard that?' Harper inclined his head. He was grinning broadly. He looked nicer for it.

'Yes,' said Wendover. 'Yes, I think we will be taking it to the others.'

'They aren't so nice when they grow up,' said Morag wistfully.

4: The Cemetery

It was bitterly cold. Wind slashed along the crippled motorway, tore at the pale vegetation, and sandblasted the crazed metalling with a constant storm of fine dust lifted from the hard shoulders and flat surrounding fields. The sky was prevalently silver-grey, against which backdrop ragged strips of charcoal cloud streamed like weed in a shallow river, flung out and smoking in two- and three-mile horsetails.

Grit stuttered and hissed against the hull of the Tuppen, which squatted inert in the south-bound carriageway, silent and scarred enough to be one of the scattered derelicts. A pylon reared above it, trailing mesh and humming in the wind. Five hundred yards ahead a desolate slip road snaked away left and was lost immediately in a freak fold of land.

Wendover, numbed to the core, stared from his position in the turret at the barely discernible mark on the horizon that was a city. Without the smoke haze of population, it was difficult to tell whether anything much remained of the place. He shifted uncomfortably, his eyes smarting with dust and swimming in warm tears that chilled as they ran down his cheeks.

Below, Arm and Harper were discussing in a desultory fashion the prospect of finding fuel in the city. They had been travelling – slowly, to avoid the wrecks – for a day and a half, and the tanks had emptied at an alarming rate. Harper was opposed to the idea, but with none of his customary vigour, possibly because he had no real basis of contention: they were impelled to go in, like it or not; the turbine would take them no further than the city before it ground to a halt. He seemed to be arguing merely to hear the sound of his own voice.

The doctor listened with a faint but mounting irritation that was directed mainly at himself: the decision was his, the correct course was dictated by circumstances; and yet he stood in the wind – his thoughts blown and buffeted about his head, his eyes straining in the abrasive air – delaying and freezing. The smear on the horizon infected him with uncertainty. It would be untenanted, except perhaps by memory, and broken; but he saw it as a definite risk.

The plagues had died down, but the centralization that had bred them remained anathema to him: there was the possibility that one of the group might pick up a hitherto dormant microbe. And on a deeper, more personal level, he was reluctant to enter the empty and decadent streets that would surely remind him of the scope of the disaster.

He tapped impatient fingers on the turret coaming. The child started to wail, emphasizing the need for action. He stepped back into the steel bowels of the wagon, careful in case he lost his footing on the worn diamond tread of the platform. It wasn't much warmer inside. He gestured wearily at Harper and the dwarf, who were cramped in the forward compartment, and said curtly, 'you can shut up now. We're going in.'

He dropped into the personnel space next to the girl. She smiled at him. She had taken her shirt off and used it to cover the child. Huddled in the half-dark, the leather jacket wrapped tightly around her, she looked frail and ill. A single shaft of grey light slanted from an open observation slit on to her face. She was humming a sort of lullaby, but the child was taking no notice; as the car lurched forward, the initial cough of the turbine vibrating the full length of the metal shell, it redoubled the volume of its cries.

'It's cold,' said Wendover, as pleasantly as he could. He had found it difficult to hold any sort of conversation with her. Not that she was withdrawn: the fault probably lay with himself. He supposed it was enough that they could communicate basics. He took off his coat, swaddled it round the noisy bundle. She nodded. She seemed a little simple-minded.

The Tuppen bucked, mounting the slip road, In an effort to dispel his misgivings about the city, he pondered the implausibility of the child: that there should be no preliminary mutation made it clear that something other than the slow and painful processes of selection had operated here (and elsewhere, too, if the girl was correct, thus invalidating any question of accident). He was then forced to define the mutation in terms of a rumour. They had pulled it off, after all. It made him wonder how many of the other myths of the disaster period were based on fact. Arm turned his ugly head and yelled over the moan of the turbo that they had arrived.

The wagon began to judder over the shattered brick of the suburbs, and the slipstream brought him a swell of brick dust and old paint through the observation slit.

Wendover stood outside a basement surgery among the lumpen Victorian perspectives at the north end of the city. Away from the centre, the streets were in surprisingly good order. Here and there a charred gap destroyed the symmetry of the parochial terraces, a black pit like one of his own dissolving teeth: but here there was nothing like the ruin prevailing in the administrative and industrial areas, where the arcades and factory complexes resembled a second Dresden.

Arm and Harper had discovered the fuel depot of a haulage firm, the meters of which registered the presence of just over a thousand gallons of kerosene located in four separate underground storage cells. They were working on the problem of getting some of it out and into the Tuppen. They would also need a means of carrying extra fuel: the girl could not be precise about the location of the mutant colony, but they had no reason to suppose the journey would be short.

Morag herself was looting thirty years late among the drapers' stores, ostensibly on behalf of the baby. Wendover had left them to it and come scavenging for the less perishable items of his profession.

The place was grim, exuding a paint-flaked seediness that he guessed to have been present well before the collapse of the city. Lichen grew on the lintels and brown stains fanned vertically down the brickwork wherever there was metal in direct contact. There were broken milk bottles in the basement area, each shard filmed with a greenish damp deposit; two slightly incongruous dustbins half full of slime that smelt less putrid than the channel outside his Nissen hut only because there was less of it; and an incoherent muddle of bones, yellowed and green-filmed at the joints, indicated that some pathetic citizen had made it thus far and no further in the days of the plague.

The weather-blistered door confounded his feeble attempts to force it, so he turned his attention to the window, a four-and-a-half-foot square of frosted and intagliated glass. The word *surgery* was engraved in large italic capitals beneath a stunted arabesque of scrollwork. It looked like the window of an Edwardian smoking room.

Avoiding the depressed tangle of bones as much as possible, he found half a brick in the area. Paused, mildly amused to discover himself savouring the prospect of vandalism.

Soaking up the silence of the street, he balanced it mentally against the crash of glass, and saw that it was good. As he hefted the brick forward, his ears caught the distant sound of a turbine: Arm, warming up the Tuppen. The faint dragonfly hum was swamped out by the brittle racket of falling glass, and by the time the splinters had stopped tinkling in the room beyond, the sound had faded.

He removed the remaining shards by running the brick round the window-frame, then climbed clumsily in, the Smith and Wesson banging heavily against his hipbone. He was delighted with himself.

Inside, it was shadowy and damp, a small dusty oubliette of a room, grimy blue wallpaper puffing limply where the moisture had got to it. Round-the-wall benches and a pile of rat-chewed pulp on a three-legged table marked it as a waiting room.

He tried the door and entered the passage outside without difficulty. The surgery door was labelled, the rest of the floor blocked by low wooden gates and – customary churlishness – signs saying ABSOLUTELY NO ADMITTANCE TO PATIENTS.

Chrome-appointed desk, shelves and chairs. A smell of rat droppings, gloom in the corners, and a foetus-shaped stain over the scales. It was dank and dusty and hadn't been disturbed for at least a generation.

He had been poking about for half an hour – finding a GP's bag, well stocked and superficially in good condition; one or two antiseptic aerosols still pressurized and operating; and the quite impossible luxury of a bottle of whisky – when he heard the turbine again, cruising down the street.

It stopped. A door slammed. The outer door of the surgery rattled.

'Try the window, Arm!' he yelled, involved via a filing cabinet of record cards in an almost

pleasant re-creation of the past. The late occupant of the place had apparently been a
homoeopath.

There was a pause. He heard a faint noise
behind him; turned jubilantly to report his major
find; caught a glimpse of a shadowy and unidentifiable figure in the crepuscular light. Then
there was an eye-searing burst of flame and a
massive pain in his left temple. Echoes hammered round his brain. He fought for reason and
attained only a dull feeling of surprise; and it
was surely unfair that he had to fight the shadows too. They stirred, leapt out of the corners of
the room, and swallowed him up.

He floundered to the surface from a vision of
an entomic Armageddon in which he partici-
pated as an armoured stick-insect with twin
revolving turrets mounting pneumatic cannon.
There were flames, and a smell of burning
chitin.

He was lying uncomfortably on his side
beneath the foetus-shaped stain; there was a
remarkable pain in his head. Blood had caked
on his scalp, but his skull seemed to be in fair
shape: his gentle prospecting fingers located a
thin elongated wound, stinging painfully, but
surrounded by no soft or depressed areas.

He crawled to the desk and got into a chair,
regarding vaguely the bottle of whisky. The
figure in the dark. Huge, wielding a sceptre of

flame. He shouldn't drink any of the spirit. This huge dark figure. And he had been shot. The stain on the wall. Drink the huge. Whisky wielding sceptre figure. I'd better warn the others.

He sat slumped for some time in a painful stupor, trying to forget the irrelevancies, then, when he felt able to concentrate on a single task, looked for the black bag. It had gone, along with one of the aerosols. He shook his head sadly, picked up the remaining spray, and blundered out of the surgery. The whisky he left. For some reason he wanted to get away from the stain on the wall. It made him feel uncomfortable.

Outside, light pricked his eyes like retinal acupuncture. The wind had risen again; it was hurling down the funnel of the street, fluting through rusted and bent television aerials. An eroded, flaking tin can was tumbling down the centre of the road, making eerie music. Dust stung his face. Boiling cumulus above the roof-ridges and toppling antennae threatened rain. One side of the unfastened raincoat fluttered with tatterdemalion vigour; the other hung lifeless at his side, ballasted by the pistol. He began to walk as fast as he could, trying to wrap the coat more firmly round him as he went. It wouldn't stay put. The clouds burst and hail battered his skull. Often, he swayed.

Dusk was approaching as he reached the fuel dump.

The wagon stood at the kerb, silent, reeking of JP4, the strange selection of cans lashed to its armour giving it an even more bulky and squat appearance. Harper slouched on the turret, his good leg bent under him, the other dangling; he was whistling and grinning at the girl, who sat below him on the engine cowling fiddling with a scrap of bright cloth. This vivid splash of tangerine was the only colour in a washed-out vista; it stood out sharply against the olive hull and dark surrounding tower blocks.

Wendover knew that he was about to pass out. He concentrated hard on the flash of orange; it was his sole point of orientation in a dimensionless world. He was a ghost among grey façades. There was no sign of Arm or the child. Harper saw him and said something to the girl.

Wendover stumbled over the kerb and fell. The cripple slid off his perch and limped up to him at a great rate. Morag followed, strip of cloth still in her hand.

'Doctor!' Harper knelt beside him, mouth tense.

Wendover coughed, mumbled; finding his voice abruptly, managed to tell them what had happened. He felt himself lifted; blacked out; came to again immediately, to find three faces hanging over him.

'Get in the car,' he muttered.

But by then it was too late. The flat crack of a heavy-gauge pistol echoed like a bursting maroon in the gloom. Something whined off the skin of the Tuppen.

Wendover, his vision bent by pain and shock, watched catwalks and fire escapes come alive with fat grey maggot figures: the surrounding walls seethed like worm-ridden corpses. After the original shot, only a faint rustling broke the silence of the advance.

Arm swarmed ape-like up the side of the car, got half in and half out of the turret, and, balanced precariously, began to use the pneumatics like a riot hose, scoring indiscriminate lines of fire across the dusk. Bedlam followed, as areas of masonry exploded into singing fragments. Morag was crouching between the wheels of the vehicle, the screaming child clutched to her and her face pinched with fear. Yelling obscenely, Harper stood over the doctor, shooting Pauce's automatic wildly off into the air.

Their fire was returned half-heartedly from perhaps three sources, wan stabs of light whose attendant concussions were masked by the continual racket of exploding cannon shells. This constant flare of shell-burst lit the scene like a stroboscope: each separate flash illuminated a brief still-shot; a gesture of fear or anger condensed and arrested; a single shot from a partial documentary. The regular flicker made sniping impossible and gave a killing edge to Arm's saturation technique. His small indistinct figure in the turret made an indifferent target.

They were a poor lot. Very few of them had guns. Some carried knives, and iron bars glinted beneath weirdly lit faces. Most of them seemed to be misshapen about the head. Wendover caught fragmentary glimpses of mutilated limbs and flapping rags as they skittered for cover under Arm's pyrotic lash.

It was the rags that gave him his first clue to their identity: here and there he saw the grubby sleeve of a black jacket, the absurd smear of a dirty white collar; and, once, a pair of pinstripe trousers hacked off in tatters at the knee.

The old hierarchy had hung on: intimately involved in centralization, unable to deal with the problems presented outside the high-rise offices, a swarm of clerks had remained after the disaster. They lived out maggoty existences in the gutted buildings, the New Administrators, scavenging the dismembered corpse of the city.

The regalia of a discontinued masonry – what meaning did it have for the starved remnants of urban man?

His gentle amusement was interrupted by a shrill cry from the dwarf.

Something glassy and glittering arced through the air from a second storey window. It fell short of the Tuppen by fifteen yards and erupted with an oily woosh of flame, scattering orange highlights and streamers of fire. Heat seared Wendover's face despite the bulwark of the armoured car. The pneumatics cut out suddenly and Arm came down the steel mounting rungs, his face contorted, fear in his eyes. He was shouting into the sudden silence. He dragged the girl from her bolt-hole, sweat shimmering on his thick bare arms.

'What . . . ?' called Harper.

'Get *out!*' screamed the dwarf, giving the girl a powerful shove with the flat of his hand. She ran off whimpering, huddling a noisy bundle to her breasts. Arm turned to the cripple, gesticulating wildly. They lifted Wendover up. He found it impossible to share their sense of urgency: he regarded the uncharacteristic and slightly absurd expression of panic on the face of the dwarf with feverish humour. There was something farcical about such a sudden reversal of fortune. He jolted through the dark, giggling.

He was sinking into a comfortable stupor when the Tuppen blew.

A second Molotov cocktail swung in a slow hyperbola from somewhere among the front ranks of the ambush. It toppled lazily, end over end – throwing out little slivers of red light as it passed over the dying, greasy flames of the first – and burst on the wagon's outer shell of fuel cans, just behind the turret.

An immense fireball bloomed as the JP4 went up: it swelled, hesitated, then doubled in size with the explosion of the car's magazine. The light became intense and white as each shell added its quota of brilliance.

Metal became paper thin, ran molten. The internal tanks burst, flinging incandescent shrapnel. A false dawn bathed the black-socketed façades, putting out the eyes of ambushed and ambusher alike.

For Wendover, the sick realization of just how much they had lost coincided with a return of darkness.

The last thing he saw was Arm, his hair and clothes burning like a torch, frantically beating at himself. The after-image of the blast hung for some time in his coma, fluorescing and changing colour.

5: The Nature of the Catastrophe

Arm the dwarf felt furnace heat on his back. Black smoke stank and writhed about him. The dark-eyed ruins were rooted and permanent: they might have been falling apart for a millennium, paradoxically ageless like Celtic keeps and medieval towers.

In front of him, stumbling backwards away from the burning machine, his long birdlike face limned with mournful unsteady Boschian light, Harper mouthed incoherently. His voice was submerged in the long slow rumble of the explosion.

Between the two of them, Wendover: his head lolled to the left, bumping Harper's arm; there was spittle on his open lips and on the sleeve of the reefer jacket. He was in a mess. He sagged like a wet sack, breathing hoarsely and with great effort, his chest heaving. His ankles were thin.

The dwarf's legs weren't up to the extra

weight, he staggered. Over Harper's shoulder he caught a quick glimpse of the girl, scuttling out of reach of the light.

The explosion had three distinct phases. Attuned to the death of light armour, he counted them: reserve fuel, yellow and almost soundless, a hot whisper; magazine, a fierce white flower, crackling; integral fuel, deeper yellow bellowing its way out of the bowels tinted with oxidizing metal salts. Boom, Boom, Boom. Huge shadows were projected on the buildings.

The light touched the back of his neck and set him on fire.

His hair crackled and blazed. In Harper's eyes he saw himself silhouetted against his own fire; flames licked along his limbs. He screamed with fright. He dropped Wendover's legs and began to beat at himself, yelling 'Help-help-help!' in a voice that couldn't be heard over the long roar of the burning Tuppen. Pain scraped at his scalp, the muscles of his shoulders, his buttocks. He fell on the floor and rolled about.

Harper loomed above him, supporting the doctor's shoulders and at the same time trying to take off his jacket. Running back through the blazing detritus, Morag wailed like a curlew, the child panicking in her arms. Harper dropped Wendover, ripped off the coat. Arm saw it descend on him like a flapping black bat. Enveloped in it, felt the flames die. He wasn't too badly hurt.

'Christ,' said Harper, 'Christ almighty.' It was all he ever seemed to say.

Arm got to his feet.

'Come on,' he muttered, grinding his teeth. 'They'll catch up . . .'

Something hit him hard in the small of the back. Turning, he found a massive distorted face hanging above him, its mouth a fixed six-inch leer, its eye-sockets empty. He took a second blow on the base of the spine, swung his fist up at the nodding horror and fell. A quiet chuckle followed him down. Blood ran from his nose and there was cold grit under his cheek.

Unable to move, he watched Harper struggling with a pack of incredible leaping things, bundles of rag and swollen carbuncled heads with white, roughly textured features. Metallic laughter rattled through the crimson dusk, but the huge faces were set like death-masks.

Harper fired his pistol once; grunted; collapsed. Morag shrieked, ran aimlessly about. Somebody kicked Arm in the head, and he dropped through a black hole in the ground.

Slanting fitfully through pale screens of cloud, the peculiar weak light of late afternoon struck up off wet tarmac, turned water droplets into mercury, and washed the drab canted flanks of the Fifth Republic armoured column as it crawled Indian file into a small Midlands town.

The rain stopped, leaving the air silvered and damp. The rumble of thunder was replaced by the steady, belling moan of turbines.

The column consisted mainly of Tuppens with a scattering of light, squat Rendell scouts jury-rigged with 50mm slow-firing cannon. The insignia of the latter were freshly painted and in certain cases still wet, green enamel running down turrets and armour.

The new Republic was forty hours old: Obtulowicz's Fourth had collapsed after an accident with a machine pistol, leaving his deputy, Hall – who had finally won over Hodgson and Innes, thus gaining a majority of one on the General Staff and, more important, control over Innes' Tactical Support Wing – to change the constitution once more. It meant no change of target: for the past month, which spanned Obtulowicz's regime and even took in a little of the Third Republic, the column had been hunting the same mixed group of Anarchist and Situationalist mobile guerillas.

A single Marsden observation vehicle, its white anti-radiation paint blistered and streaked with grime, its multiple dish antennae sweeping regularly, bumbled along five hundred yards ahead of the main body. It had been designed primarily to control tactical atomic fire in conjunction with a helicopter wing and high-level reconnaissance aircraft; but the planes were grounded by lack of fuel and even its efficiency as a ground detector-relay was impaired considerably.

The Marsden was slowing them down, and Arm was bored.

His Tuppen, a one-off job with a napalm thrower lashed to the forward plates, lay fourth in the column. Water thrown up by the wagon in front forced him to wipe his face frequently, and the dark wet patches on his uniform contrasted vividly with the faded areas where Second, Third and Fourth Republic insignia had been removed. At present, his combat jacket was featureless but for the chevrons on his left sleeve. He was attempting simultaneously to clench his teeth against the vibration of the turbo and continue a conversation with Block, his gunner.

Block, who had left his turret and was perched uncomfortably above and behind the driving seat, was a tall, sad-looking ectomorph, with eyeballs receding into his skull and an air of haunted impermanence. Prior to the breakdown of government, he had existed along the verge of society: playing something that he described as 'dirty harmonica' in a series of dingy clubs; sleeping on the floors of other people's cold-water apartments; busking in the streets – one of the urban intransigents who had come into their own with the disintegration of the system which had never really applied to them.

For the last couple of miles he had been running a plastic brush through his girly auburn hair. To little effect: the draught from the driving slot kept whipping it about his meal-coloured face.

'Your anarchists, now,' he said. '*They've* seen what's going on. The whole concept of administration is finished.' His voice was possessed of a permanent and deceptive tone of injury. 'They can see that the only way from here is down. In a year we'll have reached the Twentieth Republic, and it'll be a one-village set-up. They're just anticipating.'

Arm brushed a spider off his low-ratio lever. He didn't much care about politics.

'Put that bloody brush away. Why don't you join them if that's your scene?'

Block laughed.

'They don't get paid,' he said. His face crinkled up. He continued to brush his hair.

Brake lights flashed on the car in front. Arm stopped the Tuppen suddenly, throwing the gunner off his perch, and listened. Faint above the noise of the idling engines came a hollow clack of small-arms fire together with the heavier thump of an anti-tank projector as the Marsden located and engaged the first pocket of suburban snipers. Two Rendells detached themselves from the column, turbines shrieking, and hammered up to the skirmish area. Their Chambers cannon began pounding. The shooting died out. The column moved again, more slowly than before.

The town gave them little trouble and no aid at all; and since its reaction to the guerillas had probably been identical, nobody cared much. A few women left the streets as the observation vehicle ground past proclaiming martial law in bent Martian tones from its exterior speakers. They clutched ordinary cancerous children, who watched the guns with ordinary resentful eyes.

The shock of the breakdown had left them caught between culture gradients, wondering when normal service might be resumed. Only the few who, like Block, had recognized the situation for what it was, saw the disaster as an opportunity to enact private fantasies. The rest sat in shock, in stale living rooms, waiting for the televisions to announce it had all been patched up. They brought no mirrors, and avoided looking directly into one another's faces.

An emaciated youth stood in the dreamhole window of a clocktower in the town centre, his face featureless and suppurating. He tried to throw a home-made bomb as the column wound beneath him. As he drew back his arm, shouting somebody's name, the bomb went off. Bits of masonry rattled against the armour plate in front of Arm's driving slit. Brickdust puffed into the interior of the car.

'Who was this "Trotsky" anyway?' asked Arm.

There were a number of incidents such as this, cruel and petty: however, Arm's special weapon was needed only once before they left the place.

They were passing through the suburbs on their way out, flanked by gardens gone to waste of lupin and hollyhock. The hot pink spears of the lupins contrasted vividly with the broken windows and deteriorating paintwork of the semi-detached bungalows to which the gardens belonged.

The Marsden detected a magnetically triggered device cached in a sewer main. It stopped and disgorged a team of disposal experts wearing metal hoods and breastplates. As they deployed, one of the scout cars broke column to cover them, the figure in its turret swivelling nervously to sweep binoculars over the bungalows. They had become menacing in their silence. Arm let his motor idle and tried to imagine them pre-disaster. He was unable to do it: the gardens might always have been like this, jungles.

'Ah well,' said Block sagely, when he told him, 'ah well.' He put his brush away and went to sleep, waking occasionally to sneeze as pollen got at the membranes of his nose.

Complaining in surly voices about the weather, the engineers struggled with a manhole cover in the middle of the road. Eventually they lifted it and began warily to descend. The operation took some time. Block snored.

Off to the right, the bungalows parted around a complex of low flat buildings which had formerly housed a primary school. Fading yellow lines quartered an asphalt yard.

There was a polite cough. The lieutenant in the turret of the scout shouted in surprise: a moment later, vanished as his wagon bellowed and exploded. A crackle of rifle-fire followed the blast and two of the disposal experts remaining above ground fell across the manhole, their limbs waving awkwardly.

Several Tuppens, each burning rubber from all six wheels, moved up to the verge of the playground and began to fire steadily into the building. Absorbing something in the order of ten thousand rounds a minute, the façade quaked. It ruptured, revealing sagging floors and broken furniture. The place collapsed comically in a mushroom of dust. The Tuppens reversed away, gears crashing petulantly. Comparative silence.

From under the rubble the PIAT projector coughed again. Another wagon blew, scattering burning odds and ends. Arm nudged Block awake.

'Business as usual,' he said.

He envisaged the sniper, trapped in a sub-cellar but still belligerent. It always happened.

'You'd think they'd learn,' said Block.

Cautiously, Arm left the line and edged the wagon towards the rubble, slipping his clutch, which was hard work. A shell fizzed overhead, exploded in the road.

'Missed,' said Arm, sweating a little. 'Must of got blood in his eyes. Hey, hear that, I said . . .'

While the belligerent loaded up, Block tagged the pre-heat lever and gave the fuel time to warm.

'Turn a couple of degrees left,' he suggested, his voice muffled by the turret armour, 'and be quick.' They had to aim the whole vehicle.

He pressed the trigger. Arm slammed the driving slit shut as a twenty-yard gout of jellied petrol spewed out of the launcher under his nose, enveloped the wreckage, and ignited with a terrifying *wooomph*.

When he opened it again, everything was red and gold. A faint screaming carried over the crackle of burning timber. A patch of rubble heaved, bricks flying.

The sniper dragged himself out from under, and burned to death at the conjunction of two yellow lines.

'There you go,' said Arm.

*

North of the town, semi-industrial waste ground merged into straggling common land overgrown with nettles and fireweed. At no point was the transition abrupt. Ditches and meagre, rusty streams partitioned the heath and far off was a gleam of open water. A wet wind ruffled the dreary vegetation, whistled through the antennae of the command vehicle. Roads were bad, Arm's face smarted from the napalm job, and Block had gone to sleep again.

The column made fair progress for a time, only to be halted in the centre of the heath by a tribe of journeymen electricians and television repairmen. Their encampment spilled from a lay-by, five- and ten-hundred-weight vans, powered by the steam engines redeveloped during the mid-seventies, parked raggedly across the road.

Morose children played intricate games among themselves while the women in their long embroidered skirts and boleros cooked an evening meal over paraffin stoves. The vans had no flash-heating coils, were cold and intractable; and the tinkers seemed to enjoy persecution. They shouted and waved their arms.

The order to stop engines filtered down the line, which gave Arm's calves a rest. He adjusted the blocks on his brake and clutch pedals, then tapped his fingers aimlessly. He discussed the concept of military efficiency with himself.

95

The anarchists hit them in fading light with a strange and dislocated tactic.

A broad swathe of gorse some twenty yards off the road shuddered and snarled and fell apart. Out of it burst a ram-charged Buick saloon three generations old, burning *petrol*. Its fierce chrome grin leapt and bounded towards the column. Its coachwork was decorated with fiery swirls of luminescent paint. Thick black smoke poured from under its bonnet. At the wheel was a massive naked madman with blond hair and beard. He was laughing loud enough to be heard above the racket of the engine. Once, he bawled:

'*Live in the PRESENT!*'

The Buick made the road, its suspension sick and groaning, and at 50 or 60kph rammed the Marsden amidships. Both vehicles were absorbed in a tremendous fireball.

Simultaneously, several half-tracks and a bulldozer painted with irregular purple stripes trundled out of a drainage culvert and began to enfilade the Fifth Republic armour with obsolete wire-guided missiles.

An ancient Aston-Martin howled out of the gorse, snapped its steering linkages, and side-swiped a late-model Lewis/Phoenix done up in neo-Cubist designs. The Aston appeared to have been loaded with napalm, but the turbocar pulled through and delivered a hundredweight of ammonal to a stalled Rendell at the rear of the column.

'The *fuckers!*' screeched Block, frantically mobilizing his turret with a hand-crank. Arm injected fuel into the turbine and they got power. Others hadn't been so lucky: half the column had been taken out with turrets locked rigid. Affronted, Block shelled suicide squadrons composed of Cadillacs from museums and heavy-plant machinery from scrap-heaps.

Night came on. Old headlamps cut the dark in aimless, violent patterns.

'They use drugs, of course,' said Arm, reasonably.

By now they were skirmishing on the run, which enabled them to turn the napalm-thrower on line-of-sight targets. It gave him something to occupy his mind.

Then, up ahead, he saw a big self-centring tank, festooned with whip aerials and painted pink. A 155mm monster, it had him bracketed in no time, keeping well out of his range. Shaped charges erupted port and starboard. Jinking violently, he pitched over the heath and found the road.

He cut the power to the turret because it slowed them down, and burnt rubber taking the Tuppen into the high seventies.

'I think it's time we bugged out,' he told Block. He was worried stiff.

Block blew his nose and tracked the turret manually until they had successfully deserted.

They went to earth at dawn in a derelict cottage some distance away from the heath. It was a small building, but black and solid against the brightening sky. Behind it lay a reservoir, a hundred acres of ghostly grey water with an island and some swans. Arm ran the Tuppen off the road, down a steep clay embankment into a hawthorn copse. An occasional deep thud shook the ground.

He woke up at about midday with his face in a puddle of sunlight cross-hatched with the shadows of lath and rafter. The uneven stone floor was covered with dirty white guano, and pigeons burbled in the roof. Bits of broken, unidentifiable furniture huddled in the corners of the room, yellow with filth. Some rags and a bone lay under the multi-paned window. Block was out. It was quite peaceful.

Scratching hairy belly thoughtfully, Arm went to the window, scrubbed dust from an intact pane with the heel of his hand. Through an irregular circle edged with grime he watched Block camouflaging the armoured car, arranging branches and ivy artistically over its decks: outline broken up, it was disappearing fast. He hadn't yet begun on the ruts and skid-marks that scored the embankment. Arm yawned, cracking the joints of his fingers.

A light wind ruffled the reservoir, brought to his ears a brief, fluctuating rumble. Block heard it too, stopping to brush his pretty hair from his eyes and gaze round nervously. He muttered something and went on raping the copse.

Arm turned away and examined the furniture. He dragged some interesting pieces into the light, looked at them from different angles. The pigeons fluttered uncomfortably in the rafters, spattering him with dung. He stirred the rags beneath the window with the toe of his boot, kicked them across the room when he could make nothing of them.

The rumble returned, steadied, became independent of the wind. Block hurried to the edge of the copse, moving furtively. He looked towards the cottage and called out, but he couldn't see Arm watching him from behind the dirty window. He stumbled back into the bushes and began to tear at them.

The cottage vibrated subtly. Rotting plaster fell on Arm's head, and the pigeons wheeled away, wings clacking worriedly.

Arm cleaned another pane, to see the shuddering road better. The embankment swept up to his right like a green shoulder, topped with twisted signposts and dotted with poorly speedwell.

Along it was moving a 3,000hp tank with day-glo pink armour, its tracks bright and wide and deadly. It came on slowly and stopped. Painted in white, foot-high capitals along its flanks were the words: WHAT IS THE EXACT NATURE OF THE CATASTROPHE? Its self-centring gun was decorated with vertical black and white bars, decreasing in size towards the bulbous muzzle. Heat haze rose fore and aft from its engine louvres.

Block froze, a length of ground-ivy draped over his shoulder.

Arm cleaned another pane.

Out of the vehicle's big low turret climbed a figure in bright blue velvet trousers, a white shirt with lace ruffles, and a bottle-green jacket with silver epaulettes. Rings glinted on his fingers. His thin face was entirely without cancers, white and smooth. His shoulder-length black hair was tied back with a black ribbon. He had a wispy little beard. His feet were bare but clean. He stood on the turret looking casually from the ruts in the embankment to Block in the spinney.

He opened his coat and unhooked a small black grenade from the wide leather belt revealed. He nodded agreeably as he threw it underhand into the hawthorn. Block made a strangled, unpleasant noise. There was a sharp report, a flash, and the spinney caught fire in several places. The partial camouflage of the Tuppen blazed. Soon the whole area was a furnace.

Spattered with phosphorus from the bomb, Block ran between the trees, roaring and crying, leaping like the white and yellow flames.

Arm turned and found his way quietly to the rear entrance of the cottage. Outside, he ran as quickly as his warped legs would carry him to the edge of the water. As he lowered himself in, Block's screams were cut off by the explosion of the Tuppen. The cottage began to burn.

Arm swam out to the eyot, abandoning his standard-issue pistol and belt when they began to hamper him.

He regained consciousness in a dim cold room lined with orderly rows of books. He was lying on his stomach with his head in a draught. He didn't understand. He rolled over on to his back and winced at the pain in his neck and shoulders. Somebody he knew bent over him and touched his hands.

'I couldn't have done anything, you see,' he explained to her. 'They'd have found me.' That was very reasonable.

She nodded and gave him a drink.

A second figure moved vaguely against the background of books, muttering and running its fingers through long blond hair. He worried for a moment that it was Block come back to him. Leaping grotesques with bulbous heads danced about in his head and there were games in the gloom.

6: The Adjudicators

Harper paced the floor from *Current Affairs* to *Encyclopedias* and stood helplessly over the bodies of Arm and the doctor, his crippled leg aching rheumatically.

Before the split with Tinhouse, all his decisions had taken their dynamic from a youthfully rigid liberal code: a clumsy apparatus that was, in fact, heavily puritanical and informed only within limits: an ideal set of criteria for village life.

But the violence of the kidnapping had weakened his pose; defined the peripheries of his knowledge and experience; and left him attempting feebly to build an attitude that included the new stimuli. This process left him relying heavily on Wendover and unable to assimilate the situation in which the group now found itself.

Arm lay prostrate on the vinyl tiles a few

feet away from the doctor, his scalp scorched
hairless, the nape of his thick neck blistered.
The whole library stank of his charred clothes.

'All over!' he shouted. 'It's green! It's green!'
He moaned and made swimming motions;
twitched; lay still. He had been like this since
catching fire after the ambush, delirious. He
seemed to be reliving some incident of his past.

Morag, who had been sitting snuffling on a
reading table, got up and knelt over him, muttering small comforts. Harper went over to
them. When he found the dwarf still uncon-
scious, he suggested sourly. 'Turn him over or
something,' and went back to his pacing. Morag
began to weep again. It irritated him beyond
bearing, or so he thought.

He was more interested in Wendover, who
seemed to be in worse condition than the dwarf,
with far less cause. An examination of his head
revealed a very minor flesh wound and some
powder burns; yet he sprawled inertly over a
moraine of political journals spilt from a broken
shelf, his breathing disturbed and arhythmic.
His skin was hot and damp to the touch,
stretched over the bones like doped silk. He
looked like a cadaver. Harper watched him carefully, expecting a sign. He needed some
reassurance.

Arm grunted and turned himself over.

'Give him some water,' Harper told the girl,

without looking up from the doctor's swollen glands and skeletal face.

They had been in the library for seven or eight hours. It was almost dawn. Of the strip lights that marched in orderly rows across the high ceiling, two remained operative. The building's failing autonomic-power system — its roof-top solar cells chipped and eroded by decades of wind — made them flare and fizz erratically. Their light was lost in the immense circular expanse of the room, falling dimly on the spines of fifty thousand books. Harper shivered, thinking of lost technologies and the weight of knowledge stored around him. With the locking of the doors, he and Morag had come to an unspoken decision to remain near the entrance, unwilling to move further into the shadows of the waiting information pool.

Arm choked and said: 'I couldn't have done anything, you see. They'd have *found* me!' Catching sight of Harper, who had resumed his long walk, he flinched. 'Block, baby?' he whispered.

Harper took the tin cup from Morag and threw the remaining water into the dwarf's face.

'Wake up, Arm. We're in a mess.'

After locking them in, their captors had rushed away down the fallopian tubes of the building, singing and chanting. Later, it had been possible to hear from some distant room the drumming of feet and the hollow piping of crude wind instruments. Throughout the night they had received sporadic visits from the savages. None, however, had entered the library; they stood about in small groups – talking in stage whispers and hammering on the doors – and then ran away, like children teasing a chained dog. Harper understood none of this. For some time now the building had been silent.

He watched the dwarf clamber unsteadily to his feet, making no attempt to help him.

'You had some pretty funny dreams,' he said.

Arm frowned. He looked down at Wendover.

'Did I say something?'

'Nothing I remember, no.'

The dwarf looked pleased. He felt the pulse in Wendover's wrist; ran his fingers over the scalp wound. He picked at the dried blood under his nose.

'This is a bad thing,' he said. 'The scratch isn't half of it. He's ill from something else. Did anybody salvage his bag?'

Wendover's duffel lay on the reading table next to the sleeping child, surrounded by piles of books. These, Morag had collected during the night, between bouts of weeping; going timidly to the nearest shelf and making a great show of examining its titles. When pressed, she would admit to Harper that she could barely read, but refused to say why she was poring through the illustrated weeklies or what drew her to the brightly coloured geographical magazines.

This had irritated him more than the fits of sobbing, because although he would have genuinely enjoyed helping her to find whatever it was she was after – he wanted to demonstrate his prowess as a reader.

She fetched the bag, dawdling to touch one or two of the glossier magazines and to tuck the child more firmly into its swaddlings of tangerine cloth. It murmured fractiously.

'Get a move on!' Harper urged.

Arm grinned at her, took back the medical kit, and indicated Harper with a wagging index finger. 'All the time, mouth,' he said to her, screwing his face up and showing his revolting teeth. She gave him a quick smile.

'Don't bloody *encourage* her.' The cripple felt his voice trembling petulantly, tried for a firmer grip on his anxiety.

'That's not helping anybody,' said Arm. He rummaged in the bag, taking things out and dropping them again.

'Can you do anything for him?'

He shrugged. 'Not much. He'll have to ride it out on his own. There's antibiotics here, but I can't remember if they keep. They're pretty old. Make him swallow them anyway.'

Harper took the proffered container gingerly.

The spectre of technology rattled at him from it.

'*All* of them?' he asked.

Arm was still involved with the contents of the bag.

'Aha!' he exclaimed, producing an aerosol can. 'Eh? No, give him three.' He turned to Morag and handed her the spray can. 'You can fix me up with this, I think.'

He stripped off the rags of his op-art trousers and Fair Isle sweater. His legs were thin and white and badly buckled, his torso ridiculously broad and matted with hair.

Harper stared at the twisted, immature legs, thinking that the dwarf must spend a great part of his effort merely in getting around.

Arm met his gaze, grinning.

'Fuck off and give him the tablets, eh?' he suggested.

Harper blushed. 'Sorry,' he muttered.

Morag began to spray Arm's blisters. Once she got used to the can it delighted her.

The fluorescents went off a few minutes later, and weak pink light filled the library. Harper limped to the nearest window, but all he could see was a waste of high-risers, lit up in the wan dawn. Some hours later they had a visitor.

The library had warmed up a little, Harper, still trying to get on top of things was theorizing.

'They're primitives,' he suggested. 'They have no technology left at all.'

Arm shook his head. The anaesthetic in the aerosol had slowed him down.

'They know what to do with a lock.'

'That's tradition,' Harper said, more emphatically than he had intended, because he had expected the dwarf, from his standpoint as a mechanic, to agree. 'Like a ritual,' he pressed. 'Handed down. Lock turns, paraffin burns – it isn't creative.'

'Who is?' Arm asked quietly. 'Tinhousers?'

Hurt, Harper turned away and stared at the shelf labelled *Scientific Periodicals*. 'Go to hell,' he muttered, admitting it.

Arm laughed.

'It's Pauce's con, not yours,' he said, not unsympathetically. 'He sees himself as the last civilized man, but he's just another scavenger. Anyone can read a Geiger, but the technology of it is something else.'

'So what do we use as a yardstick?'

'Do you need one? Heavy thinking isn't much use these days.'

Harper found this attitude inexplicable: both Arm and the doctor possessed bits of the old knowledge, but neither of them seemed to act from anything but impulse.

'But how do we *deal* with them, without it?' he demanded plaintively.

Arm sent his chair scuttling across the floor like a worried crab, came upright with his lips curling back off his teeth. Sweat appeared on his forehead. He did something that might have been a laugh.

Harper, upset by his wide eyes, froze. Slowly, he reached for the pistol he had lost during the ambush. Across in *Encyclopedias*, Morag dropped the tin cup. She whimpered, big eyes fixed on the dwarf. The cup bounced energetically over the vinyl, clattering, and woke the child.

Time dilation: it took half an hour for Harper to reach his feet.

Arm looked up at him. 'There's a fair possibility they'll deal with us,' he said. He showed his teeth.

The key rattled in the lock again, and something put a shoulder to the panels of the door. Bolts were drawn.

The door opened part-way, and stopped. A huge bulbous head poked through the gap, stared straight ahead for a moment, and then began to swing ponderously from side to side. It was yellow, with fat, leering lips and a bent Roman nose the size of a hand. Great dun-coloured tumors studded the lines of its cheekbones, grisly muttonchops. It was rigid and expressionless, like the face of a dead animal.

Morag wailed and grabbed Harper's hand.

(He was surprised by the gratification this produced. He forgave her for the weeping and the glossy magazines.)

The door opened fully on a strange miscegenation, the disgusting head was set on narrow, stooped shoulders. There seemed to be no neck. A thin, pot-bellied body twitched beneath it, dressed in dirt-glazed black coat, grey and ragged woollen waistcoat, and grey striped trousers cut off just above the knee. The feet were bare, the vee of chest revealed by the waistcoat covered with wiry white hairs. On the left lapel of the coat was pinned a small bright rectangle of orange plastic. The huge head swung slowly to a stop, fixed on the group in *Current Affairs* like a queer gun turret.

'Paper mâché,' mused Arm. Then: 'Bloody hell, it's a *mask*.'

This information changed nothing. An uncomfortable tic began in Harper's left eyelid. He hoped it didn't show. He found himself squeezing the girl's hand.

Decisively, the disturbing figure stepped forward, placed the reading desk between itself and the group, and chanted in an old, petulant voice: 'Since you have applied for a position with this organization, you must take the preliminary tests.' It coughed dryly, fluttered its fingers to its little plastic badge.

'Look here,' Harper began, 'I'm not sure I understand any of this. We didn't want to come . . .'

'Quiet, *if* you please.' The cough again, more bronchial this time. 'I am Grocott Personnel.' Tapping the lapel badge and pausing significantly. 'I shall adjudicate the examination and assign graduates to their respective sections. You may talk softly among yourselves until we are ready to begin. Get to know one another, eh? Heh, heh. Eh?'

Harper's precarious understanding of the situation was slipping away. A sense of unreality stole over the library like fog.

'Are there any questions?' recited Personnel.

Harper said, 'Why have we been . . . ?'

A nod of the monstrous head.

'It will be very pleasant having benefits from our organization, young man. If you have the right attitude there is a pension every week. We had one just last night.'

Grocott Personnel chuckled paternally.

'Have to work your way up to it, of course.'

'You'll get nothing from him,' murmured Arm from Harper's side. 'Just shut up and watch.' He indicated the door.

Through it came three more grotesques, their masks smaller and less elaborately foul than Personnel's. The first of them – his skull daubed with some black, glistening substance to represent hair – held in one hand a bundle of short, carved sticks; the third carried a large, padded swivel chair – his face was dark ochre and flaking.

They nodded to Personnel, gave him his chair, put the papers down in front of him, and began to collect reading tables from different parts of the library. Having noisily arranged these in a block of four facing Personnel's desk, they placed a piece of paper and a carved stick carefully on each table. They worked without speaking, each one checking the efforts of the other two until satisfied.

Personnel got out of his chair and scrutinized the result, his hands clasped behind his back, his head nodding forward. He changed the position of one of the curved sticks, moved a desk an inch to the left, admonished the aide with the hair.

'*Two* inches, young man!' he snapped. 'You are not cultivating the correct attitude. It may lead to a cut in benefits. Most important to treat official equipment with respect!'

He turned to Harper.

'Be seated,' he said, 'go on, be seated do!'

Harper – unaware that he had thrust his lower jaw forward and shifted his weight on to his good leg – ignored him. The dwarf tugged at his sleeve, looked up with a grim face. 'Don't make any waves,' he warned. 'The old sod's serious about it.' He steered Harper to a chair and made the girl sit beside him.

'And the other,' said Grocott Personnel impatiently, waggling his finger at the comatose Wendover.

'He doesn't feel so good,' Arm explained. 'He can't move.'

Personnel clicked his tongue, the sound muffled behind the mask. He gestured to the aides, who picked Wendover up and sat him in the back row. His head rolled back. He groaned and muttered. Something in the fever caused him to wave his arms.

The aide with the hair stepped back, said, 'Wrong attitude,' and hit him in the face. An ulcer burst. He choked, and his eyes flickered open. He slumped and was still.

Harper began to tremble. He felt sick. He got up quickly, clenching his fists.

'Save it,' Arm recommended in a thick, unpleasant voice, forcing him down into his chair. 'Unless you want us all in the same hole. Save it for later.'

Grocott Personnel rapped his desk.

'I shall explain this once,' he said, 'and once only. During the examination period you will remain silent.

'During the examination period there will be no collusion between examinees.

114

'During the examination period, you will remain in your seats.

'The decision of the adjudicator is final.'

He made some adjustments to the set of his mask. It tilted a little, nodded sideways at a suggestive angle, then tipped back into position.

'Try to answer all questions as concisely as possible.

'Remember that the good wishes of the entire organization are with you.

'You have fifteen minutes, and you may begin.'

Eyeing the scarred fists of the ushers, Harper gave up and put his head in his hands.

Before completing this form, you should have read the advice contained in the supplementary booklet 'SOCIAL CONDITION', paying particular attention to paragraphs 8 and 9. Do not attempt to complete this form unless you have previously completed forms GKC/004 and -5. Any information given on this form will be regarded as a signed statement on the part of the applicant: *remember that there are severe penalties for misinformation.* Answer all the questions on this form unless you are supporting one or more dependants (see appended information-sheet).

BLOCK ONE

Full name of applicant .... Liability No ....

Nationality of male parent .... Liability No ....

Nationality of female parent .... Liability No ....

Have you undergone any State Registered form

of Further Education ....

State your Qualifications (if any) ....

.... (BLOCK CAPITALS ONLY)

N.B. *BLOCK ONE answers will be treated as invalid where Liability Numbers are unstated.* Your number can be obtained from your local Ministry of Liability & Intent office upon production of your MCBS card or Social Registry card.

During the examination period Harper sat morosely in front of his piece of paper, listening to small creakings in the silence and reflecting that the dwarf had no guts. Upon discovering that the stick was in fact a pencil, not very sharp, from which alternate bands of wood had been ritualistically shaved, he wrote: 'Arm for christs sake' on the form, hoping for a chance to pass it to him. But Personnel paced the desks, peering over shoulders and clicking his tongue irritably, his aides inviting quiet by example.

At one point he actually peered at the message to Arm. He nodded his terrible head sagely and patted Harper's shoulder. Expecting a blow, Harper stiffened, but nothing happened.

After above twelve minutes Wendover woke up.

'Vanessa!' he shouted.

He was staring wildly about, licking his bloody lips nervously, his throat working. His eyes were dilated. His cheek was smeared with white matter from the burst ulcer. 'There's no *need!*' he pleaded. He embraced the air, his old body jerking. He tried to free himself from the desk, succeeded only in shuffling his chair back a fraction.

With a clatter of feet, the ushers hurled themselves at him, crying: 'Wrong attitude! The wrong attitude!' The desk tipped over, pinning him to the floor. They hauled him out. Two held his arms while the third hit him repeatedly in the diaphragm with both fists.

Harper scrambled out of his desk, picked up a chair, and threw it at them. They fell in a heap, dragging Wendover ('Vanessa!' he howled) down with them, punching and biting and scratching him. Harper ran to the nearest of them and began to kick his stomach, feeling his boot hook under ribs. Wendover's delirium faded, he mewled once, and the struggle became silent.

'There will be *no* talking during the examination period!' said Personnel. 'Stop this at once!'

Harper, who had stopped kicking to brush

hair out of his eyes, watched him drag a cumbersome pistol from his coat pocket. He stood very still and allowed the ushers to pinion his arms. The scuffle had not dislodged their masks.

'I warned you, baby,' said Arm, almost reflectively.

'Your time is up,' announced Personnel.

He went round collecting the papers – stooping for Wendover's, which had a dusty bootprint on it – and, having tucked them into his waistcoat, went to the door. There he paused and jerked his head at the ushers. He said: 'Bring him.'

Harper was manhandled to the exit. He had sprained his left wrist in throwing the chair. He sneered as he passed the motionless dwarf, feeling betrayed. The baby's screams echoed from *Encyclopedias*.

7: The Attitude That Counts

Out in the corridor, with Grocott Personnel walking ahead.

Two of the aides held Harper's arms, the other came on behind them, carrying the padded swivel chair.

Harper let his game leg buckle, thrusting most of his weight on to the left-hand captor and setting him up for a kick in the groin, which he delivered with his heel. The resulting confusion – all three of them grabbing out at once, mixed up into one bemused entity – enabled him to tear free, swing round, and apply a cruel twist to the first arm that came within reach. This he broke, hammering at the reversed elbow joint with his fist. He took hold of a greasy flaking head, forced it down to knee-level with both hands, and was about to drop-kick it when Personnel stuck the pistol in his kidneys.

'Just keep them away from me!' he shouted, shoving the head viciously away from him.

Personnel clicked his tongue.

'My dear boy,' he said, 'a word to the wise, a word in your ear.' He steered Harper away from the aides with pressure from the muzzle of the gun. 'Enormous potential!' he chuckled excitedly, scrabbling in his waistcoat, but keeping the pistol steady. He produced Harper's piece of paper, waved it, and pointed to the pencil scrawl.

'You're mad,' said Harper, breathing heavily, massaging his tender wrist.

'Just a little preliminary hearing, an informal feeling-out' – Rapidly indicating himself, the corridor and Harper – 'as it were. With the right attitude' – tapping his mask significantly – 'you could go far. There might,' he whispered, 'even be a seat on the board. The benefits that might accrue, the salaries!

'Just a word to the wise. I can be a lot of help to you.' He waved his gun at the library doors. 'Off you go. Give it some thought. Take as much time as you like, ha ha.' He patted Harper's shoulder and pushed him through the doors.

Morag was suckling the child in *Current Affairs*, a silly, oblivious smile on her face changing just enough to include him as he walked in. He felt murderous. He went over to Arm, who was wiping the doctor's messy face with a wet rag. (Wendover stirred, muttered, 'Try the window, Arm . . .') A startled expression crossed the dwarf's face. He grinned.

'What happened?'

'I wrote something on the paper. I think they're all mad. I don't understand any of it. Personnel made me some sort of offer.'

Arm squeezed the rag. Water pattered on the vinyl.

'It's a step in the right direction. Now we can . . .'

'Yes,' said Harper. 'Arm, you're gutless.'

The dwarf's smile vanished. He threw the rag down at Harper's feet. 'Haven't got the point, have you?' he murmured. He stalked off, took up one of Morag's magazines and looked at the pictures.

Wendover moaned. Harper looked down at the limp body. The bivalence of their relationship was obscured and simplified by the reversal of roles.

Separated from a party of Tinhousers foraging for building materials in the abandoned back gardens of the suburbs, he wandered into an area that had been devastated when the legendary Fifth Republic – under Hall, the last true Premier – had gathered its waning strength and wiped out Bruton's Situationalists, a year before its own defeat by entropy. He knew this only as a series of bedtime stories in which Bruton was cast as Old Nick and entropy as lack of paraffin.

The event had taken place a year after his birth, and he was eleven.

It was raining again, and a cold wind sliced through his thin clothes. He shivered constantly, but was pleased by his find: he had never seen desolation on such a grand scale before, being used to the meanness of the village.

Three or four acres of demolished streets surrounded him on all sides, isolated spurs of masonry fingering up from the rubble. *Nick Bruton brought up his Cadilacs, but Hall was wise to that.* The ragged skyline gave him a strange feeling of security. Occasionally, he would come upon an almost intact row of houses, their windows starred and crazed, rotting curtains flapping in the wind. *Bit by bit Old Nick's snipers fell back. Oh, they hid all right, but Hall was wise to that.* At these times he walked jauntily in the middle of the road, imagining the town to be alive again, his collar turned up against the palpable curtains of rain that blew in from the north. *So Nick called up his armour, and Hall was wise to that one, too.* Doors banged and creaked aimlessly, startling him.

In one of these areas he found the forecourt of a garage, its concrete scored by the imprints of tracked vehicles. *And at the Watford Gap, Old Nick himself got took out. He had a great big tank, but the Air Arm stopped his tricks.* He wandered round the pumps for a while, picking up rusty nuts and bolts and nurturing a fantasy in which he discovered a paraffin cache and thus escaped a beating. In the end the wind drove him into one of the houses.

But you can't keep Old Nick Bruton down. He rattles the doors when the lights go out. He'll have your *skin, me lad.*

The place was silent and oppressive, full of rubble and broken boards. Fawn shafts of light filtered through the dust that he stirred up as he moved. In the kitchen, he found some tins of food (he assumed it to be food), their labels missing. A large white refrigerator stared bleakly at him, and, when he opened it, stank. Everything was very still. The kitchen window looked out over a waste of brick where nothing moved. On the other side of it was a shopping arcade with plate-glass frontages. He put the tins in his pocket and let the smell from the refrigerator drive him out through the window.

The rain had stopped. He waded the talus of crumbling brick, stopping here and there to examine pieces of rusty metal or to listen to the chilly hiss of the wind. The bell-like grind and slip of broken tiles beneath his boots echoed distantly from the peripheral buildings. Whole people were buried under here, bones and clothes. Negotiating a drumlin of concrete from under which protruded a thing that might have been drain-pipe or gun-barrel, he slipped and fell. The earth shifted, dust and sand spewed from cavities the rain couldn't reach. He rolled down a scarp of brick, and when he reached the bottom his right leg was stuck under a balk of concrete four feet square. He wet himself.

The pain was intense when he tried to tug the leg out, and he fainted.

A movement among the rubble. He opened his eyes. Standing above him was a figure in bright blue velvet trousers, a white shirt and lace ruffles, and a bottle-green jacket with gold-braided pockets. Rings glinted from his fingers, one of them bearing an insignia of eight little radial arrows. His thin face was entirely without cancers, white and smooth. His shoulder-length black hair was tied back with a cerise ribbon. He had a wispy beard. His feet were bare and clean.

'There's a thing,' he said.

He considered the lump of concrete, massaging his beard. He bent down and embraced it; grunted; and it came up in his arms. He staggered a couple of feet and dropped it.

'Fucked my gear and no mistake,' he muttered pettishly, brushing energetically at the mud on his coat.

Harper drifted off again.

He was alone, but the weight was definitely off his leg. He dragged himself a short distance over the rubble, his mouth hot and dry. It made his head spin. His leg felt huge, pulsing. He waited for a long time, watching the shadows of individual bricks shift with the sun. Would he die? A brown bird landed nearby and nagged at him. It was almost evening when he heard unsteady footsteps close at hand.

He asked for help in a clogged, sticky voice, and hardly heard himself.

This time it was a little man dressed in a gabardine raincoat belted with string. Under its patina of cancers his face was red with exertion. There was a hunted, narrow set to his veined blue eyes. He was carrying a large plastic television console with anodized gold knobs. Over his shoulder was slung a bulging duffel-bag. Seeing Harper, he started, tripped, and dropped the television. He fumbled in his pocket, then said, 'After all, it's only a boy. What's the trouble?'

Harper wept with relief.

'Hurt meself, mister.'

'Then it's a doctor you want?' He sniggered to himself, then laughed outright, revealing brown, rotting teeth. He leant forward. His breath smelt. 'So. A doctor is it?' He snapped his fingers. 'And afterwards, eh?' He prodded a finger at Harper's breastbone. 'One of us is lucky, at least.' That pleased him too.

He examined the damaged leg, his fingers quick and precise.

'Better find some splints,' he said. Then, suddenly: 'How'd you like to learn medicine? I know you don't know what it means. Just keep still a minute.'

It took Harper five years to separate the two men in his mind.

They spent three days in the library. At dawn each day one of Personnel's aides appeared at the door with coarse bread, pigeon meat and a piece of paper; chanted: 'Benefits, sign here. Unemployed tradesmen, right-hand counter. Semi-skilled opportunities for the right man . . .' and then went away again.

The penicillin took effect on Wendover: his periods of delirium grew shorter and less frequent. On the second day he slept normally, and when he woke was quite coherent. He dosed himself from the duffel-bag, inquired after the child, but offered no advice. He ate nothing and seemed to take no interest in his surroundings.

Harper avoided Arm, speaking only when necessary. The dwarf, for his part, was amiable, but much given to reading (preferring, like Morag, the illustrated weeklies and colour magazines from *Current Affairs*). He explored the library, making frequent trips to *Music* and *Fiction N-Z*. After some of these jaunts Harper caught him grinning quietly to himself in a curiously satisfied manner.

The child made less noise. Discovering that

Morag had not named it, they discussed the matter heatedly, agreeing to nothing.

Harper got an interview with the chairman of the Board.

Personnel came into the library, drew his pistol, and sat in his swivel chair. His aides penned the group into *Encyclopedias*, isolated Harper, and worried the rest into a corner. He offered Harper a printed sheet and a pencil.

'Sign here,' he demanded.

Uncertain, Harper hesitated.

'*Write* something on it!' Arm's voice cut urgently above the hiss of the rain on the library windows. There was a thudding sound and a grunt.

Harper took the pencil and wrote: 'Let us out of hear, bastards.'

'Splendid! Splendid!' applauded Personnel. He got behind the cripple and prodded him with the automatic.

The corridors were dim and musty. The rain slashed at intact windows, formed pools beneath broken ones. The sky was full of fast-moving clouds, the light weak and grey. Personnel's lurching footsteps were muffled and anechoic as he propelled the interviewee forward. Harper gave up the idea of resistance quite early on. They passed ceiling-high murals of mould-muted tones and vaguely suggestive shapes;

doors marked CLAIMS, SUPERANNUATION, and POLICIES ONLY; a lift shaft whitened with bird-dung, choked with steel cables and obviously used as a midden; a stairwell labelled GROUND FLOOR AND OUT. At one point the passage had subsided, and they waded through a pool of brackish water.

Personnel brought him to a standstill outside a door marked SENIOR BOARDROOM and knocked lightly. He appeared to be ill-at-ease.

'Great concession to waive standard procedure like this,' he gabbled. 'You understand? He'll see you now. Remember, it's the attitude that counts. Heh heh.'

Harper fidgeted.

'Come in,' said a faint voice.

The room was painted soft blue, its walls covered with ancient, wrinkled graphs and flow diagrams. A deep-piled carpet and velvet window drapes exuded a slight smell of wet rot, their colours indeterminate. It was furnished with a large leather-topped table, across which crawled acid-blue mildew, and two velvet arm-chairs surrounded by piles of their own stuffing. On a side table stood a green-filmed bottle of water and two porcelain cups.

The chairman of the board wore a head the colour of rolled oats, perhaps twice the size of Personnel's and wider at its chipped and peeling ears than his chest. It was attached to his shoulders by an ingenious arrangement of extensions and harness, the shoulder-pieces apparently sprung and clamped to him. Perpetually smiling and puffy-featured, it swayed back and forth as he breathed. Two hanks of dun hair – one on the chin and the other swept back from a bald forehead covered with cysts arranged in simple circular patterns – had been painstakingly anchored into the papier mâché. Neither looked very convincing. The whole contrivance was covered with thick, cracked varnish.

More than ever, Harper was tempted to believe that the laws of reality were somehow suspended here, held at bay as they had been for his entire time in the city by the laws of form and procedure; handwritten laws. He had never lived in this world, he was too young.

The chairman sprang up from his chair and bounced round the desk on the balls of his feet, head teetering dangerously. Grasping Harper's hand firmly, he shook it up and down and shouted:

'I'm Senior Boardroom . . . !' And when the amazed cripple said nothing, still wondering how this fantasy had managed so long to survive the grim reality outside: 'The administrator. Senior Boardroom the administrator! Go away, Grocott, please do.'

Personnel inclined his head precariously and left.

'Now.' Boardroom settled Harper in the chair that faced the desk. 'Have a drink, old boy?' Harper glanced at the slimy bottle. He shook his head.

'Why am I here?' he asked.

Boardroom sat himself on the edge of the desk. He moved very slowly and carefully, hand to his head. His calf brushed Harper's knee, and he scratched at the straps under his armpits. He picked up a sheet of flimsy and considered it.

'Well now.' He rested his hand on Harper's shoulder. 'None of us get any younger. Running this place, keeping the increments under control: it's a job for (how shall I put it?), well, for a *fit man.*'

He gave a coy little shrug. 'Not that I *feel* old: up at six, never stuck for an idea. But' – lowering his voice – 'I'm afraid that old Personnel's not very gay. A head for figures (I can't deny that) but not much else there. I need a new man, energetic. Sure you're comfortable in that chair?'

He reached for the flimsy again. 'Now this' – indicating the scratchy *Arm for christs sake* with a very clean fingernail – '*this* shows promise. Real aptitude.' With a quick, convulsive movement his fingers came to rest in Harper's palm. Tapped it emphatically. 'We could get together, old boy. Eh? I expect you'd like to get ahead. We could work a nice one up for you quite quickly, something like Personnel's. Very nice. Well? How to put it? My experience and your *drive*?'

Suddenly Harper had the whole pitiful thing confirmed for him: a sick, dark, sad charade run by old men, for comfort. The offer made him shake. He tried to free his hand, but Boardroom's fingers had somehow enclosed his, trapping them both in the fantasy. And that wasn't all of it.

'Look,' he tried, 'I just don't want . . .'

Boardroom disengaged his hand and placed it reassuringly on the cripple's knee. 'So who needs to rush it? We have . . .' He began to massage the knee gently, swaying his head from side to side.

'Every young man wants to get ahead,' he murmured. 'Think about it.'

'No,' said Harper. He had made a mistake. He thought he could see a pair of glistening eyes through the flaring nostrils of the huge pocked nose. The hand pinched his thigh.

'No!' he yelled.

He threw himself backwards, upsetting the chair. Boardroom came down on top of him. The eyes behind the mask glittered at him. Boardroom tittered. Harper pushed vainly at his lumpy body.

'Get off!' he cried. He hit out at the mask. The nose broke off and he caught a glimpse of a

white eyebrow, a pink forehead, before Boardroom howled and clamped a hand over the tri-
angular fissure, as if his own flesh had been
damaged.

He wriggled from underneath. Boardroom
sobbed. Harper swung a fist into his spine,
kicked out wildly at the whinnying mask, and
ran out into the corridor.

'Good,' said Arm, when he heard. He didn't seem
to be worried.

Harper's lungs were full of acid from the flight
down empty passages, hunted by images of pursuit. He was wet and stinking: he had fallen into
the subsidence on SUPERANNUATION corridor. He
cast agonized glances towards the library doors:
by now, Personnel must have found the
chairman.

'We'll have to go *now*,' he said miserably
(finishing the tale and aware that he came out
of it with no credit).

'And you could find the staircase again?' asked
Arm, offering no help.

He nodded his head.

'Right then. Get the things together . . .' His
voice authoritative and unconcerned with Harper's personality problems. '. . . But take your
time.' He hurried off to *Fiction N-Z*, leaving the
cripple no wiser.

They couldn't wake the doctor. Harper threw

things into the duffel-bag, harried Morag and
the child unmercifully. Arm came back whistling. He was spinning the cylinder of Wendover's Smith & Wesson. 'Don't hurry,' he said. 'We
really need another gun.'

'Where the hell did you get that?'

He grinned slyly. 'Nobody thought to check
whether they'd taken it off him. It was still in
his raincoat. I found it just after I came round.'
He tapped the muzzle against his teeth. 'Look,'
he said, 'this thing between us is stupid. I let
them hit the doctor because I was waiting for
something like this. Somebody had to accept
their con and discover the layout of the place.
You write better than me.'

'Oh.'

'Forget it. You weren't as thick as this when
we set Pauce up with the doctor.' The grin got
wider. 'Anyway, somebody had to be the patsy.'

From the corridor came sounds of running
feet. Dislocated shouts from three or four throats
filtered into the reference section. Arm, making
his way to the door, called back over his
shoulder:

'Don't come on guilty with me, Tinhouser. It's
not my business. Here's our other gun. Just keep
yourself to yourself and don't blow this one.' His
face twitched. He liked his fun.

A moment later Personnel's crew burst into
the room. There was a quick, indistinct motion

on the part of the dwarf and the first two through, their legs knocked from under them, sprawled on to the vinyl. Harper went up and put his boot into the side of a head. His wrist still hurt. Something whined nastily past his face: wary Personnel had stuck his gun round the door before entering. Arm let him get off the one round, then rapped his hand with the Smith & Wesson. He knelt and came up with a weapon in each fist. Things went quiet.

'I told you not to interfere. Watch this bugger while I go and make some trouble.' He shoved the S & W at Harper, skittered apelike off to *Music*. There he fired Personnel's gun at something. There was a sizzling sound, then a crackle of flame. He came back, marshalling Morag on the way.

'I set the sheet-music on fire,' he told Harper. 'They can't afford to have this floor alight. Too much fuel. With care we can make it out while they're containing it. You may have trouble with the doctor.'

Harper went over and got his hands under Wendover's armpits. Wendover sat up suddenly. He looked round, seeing somewhere else; coughed and choked as smoke rolled out of *Music*; engaged finally with reality.

'You'll have to carry me, I'm afraid,' he said.

They brought Personnel along, but left his aides. Morag took Wendover's feet, having slung

the child on her back with a halter of torn
clothing, and they went furtively down the corridor, Arm impelling Grocott Personnel with his
pistol. Harper noted CLAIMS, SUPERANNUATION,
and POLICIES ONLY, paused at the derelict lift-
shaft. They were already on the staircase when
the passage shook and Senior Boardroom – hand
over his face and leading a complement of
trainee managers and beneficiaries almost as
large as the one that had destroyed the Tuppen
– whooped past in the direction of the library.
Smoke had begun to fill the corridor like a fluid
counterpart of the fungus murals.

The stairs were long, but untenanted. They grew
tired quickly and took short rests every five or
ten minutes, occupying easily defensible mid-
floor landings. Crossing a minor cascade of rain-
water that splashed down the eighteenth flight,
Morag slipped. Wendover, comatose again, slid
down to the next floor on his back, Harper
following him at a weird, stilted run, grabbing
at his shoulders. He was unhurt, but it unsettled
them all. Later, they came upon the skeletons of
some dead family of landing-dwellers, scattered
across the stairs by a mad hand. Towards the
bottom there was more evidence of these strange
squatters – artifacts constructed from old cans
and vehicle accessories, patches blackened by

fire, mosaics and middens in alcoves. They saw
no one and were glad to leave.

Outside, it was still cloudy, but the wind had
dropped.

They stood in the shadow of the tower block
that housed the library, shivering and gazing up
at its immense bulk. Concrete load beams
tapered away in sharp perspective to the place
where smoke hung like a miniature cloud round
a mountain-top, and beyond even that.

Behind them, the roads were quiet, full of
burnt-out and corroded vehicles. At junctions
the road signs stood still.

'Let's go,' said Harper, uncomfortable in the
enormous shadow.

Arm shook his head. 'Wait a minute. We don't
need this' – indicating the hostage, who was
snivelling and trying to regain the comfort of
the entrance lobby – 'any more. I want to see the
real Grocott Personnel.'

He hooked a foot behind the unfortunate
clerk's knees and brought him down. He hacked
at him with the muzzle of the pistol, tearing
open the black jacket and raising a bright red
weal on the exposed chest.

'Don't hit sick blokes,' he explained.

Personnel whimpered from a great distance
behind his mask.

Reaching down with hooked fingers, the dwarf

tore at the papier mâché of the mask where the damp journey down the stairs had weakened it. Gobs of it collected beneath his fingers, and he quickly made a sizeable hole. Personnel writhed away and tried to cover himself, his hands shaking, his mind still set on the sanctuary of the building. Arm rapped his hands with the gun, grabbed them and held on as they flew away from the smashed head.

'Oh,' he said. 'He looks just like anybody else.'

They began to walk in what seemed to be a good direction. Soon the building became one among many.

8: The Initial Contact

Ragged spinneys lined the motorway, growing denser as they travelled south. Harper led the party down the dismal perspectives, his limp pronounced after days of walking, his body twisting at each step. Stiff and uninformative, he walked in silence a few yards ahead of the other two, his hands toying constantly with the mechanism of Personnel's automatic (Wendover had taken back the S & W, and refused stubbornly to have it leave his pocket again). His face was closed and lined, the predatory look of his nose accentuated by the animal weariness in his eyes. The reefer jacket, in a mucky state, hung open as he moved; most of its chrome buttons were missing. He resembled one of the crows that flew untidily between the trees. Now and then his glance strayed to the pistol. He always seemed surprised to find it there.

Arm and the girl were pulling a small crude handcart, mismatched boards lashed together over the axles of a set of pram wheels. The wheels were buckled, they squeaked rhythmically. Slumped over the boards among a sad detritus of cooking utensils which set up their own sad counterpoint to the threnody of bent wheels was Wendover's sick body. His feet overhung the tail end of the cart. His eyes were closed.

Above them, the sky raced grey and heavy. The child wailed from a jury-rigged frame on the girl's back, its thin cries competing with the wind like gull-cry over the melancholy hiss of the tide. Neither Arm nor Morag said very much.

Harper was tired. They had spent a week in the wastes of the city, hiding from the savages and haunted by the still white columns of the high-risers on the horizon. Wendover's improvement had turned out to be short-lived: in a peeling terrace they had listened despondently to his delirium, attempting to quell both this and the crying of the child whenever the sound of distant voices drifted on the wind. It had rained continuously.

Four days ago, when the old man had shown no signs of improvement or of any desire to heal himself, they had left furtively, huddling down alleys in the early morning. Since then, Harper had given the greater part of his attention to their surroundings, hoping to avoid any repetition of the fiasco at the fuel dump. Morag could not be precise about their position. When asked, she pointed vaguely south. At least they were out of the madhouse; in an environment he knew, he felt more self-assured.

Sick as he was, Wendover remained the driving force of the group, treating Harper's tentative ascendancy as a temporary measure. Even in the depths of his fever, he had not lost sight of their objective. Once out of the city, he too had grown stronger, as if the place had exerted some tangible influence on all of them. The head wound had begun to heal, the inflammation decreasing, and his reedy voice had become the real power in the frequent disagreements on direction and speed. On the road, he lolled across the cart, his limbs slack, his face vacant: but as soon as the cripple called a halt, he would recover some of his old petulant energy. He drove them on as if racing against some private internal clock. Harper, unconsciously imparting something of the mystic to his conception of the doctor, found himself wondering if Wendover foresaw his own death.

Behind him, the creaking of the wheels stopped abruptly. It was nearly evening: he had already noted a minor but discernible change in the quality of the light around the spinneys, almost as if shadows were creeping out of them. Trees weaving their own shrouds, he thought.

He studied the area immediately in front of him with care, looking for shadows that were no part of the vegetation. It had become a ritual aimed at expiating his nonsense in the library. Satisfied, he turned to stare at the two motionless figures by the cart. He limped back to them.

Morag, squatting on the cracked macadam, had her shoe off and was inspecting her heel. Arm stood a couple of yards away, his head bowed with weariness. The dome of his skull was angry red where the scalp had been scorched. His raggy clothes fluttered in the wind. The explosion had not bothered him so much as the loss of the Tuppen; footbound, he was inefficient; indeed, since their escape, he seemed to have lost his energy and was content most of the time to take his direction from the cripple.

Morag's heel was sore and blistered.

'I can't walk any further,' she said, as Harper stood over her admiring the relaxed curve of her body. 'Not today. And it needs feeding.'

Absently, her eyes fixed on him, she replaced the shoe. Her expression softened when she looked at him, something in the eyes, the set of the head. He wished the business were that simple. He wondered briefly if a corresponding change occurred in his own features, the smoothing off of angles hardened by the wind. He doubted it. The journey had added lines to her face, and a sharp, pinched look beneath the ulcers. She was more attractive than most. He helped her up and they embraced, clumsy because of the child. Its odd, ugly face confronted him over her shoulder. He grimaced at it, and it ignored him.

'Then we'll stop. Arm?' He released himself. 'See if you can find a patch of open ground in one of the coverts. Not too far in, but out of sight of the road.'

Arm shuffled off, a quaint, rolling figure in the naked wind. There was nothing about his bearing to suggest either his earlier incisiveness or a bent for violence: crisis out of the way, he seemed to have reverted to a chrysalid stage.

Harper studied the doctor. He was asleep, his mouth gaping open. At the outset of the journey he had been, according to the cripple's reckoning, something like fifty-eight years of age. Two weeks on the road had finished the job his cenobitic existence had begun: he was an old, old man. He woke, purple-veined eyelids flickering uncertainly over the pale eyes.

'We've stopped.'

He sounded like an ancient child deprived of a promised treat. Harper felt a quick surge of irritation, but all he said was: 'It's late. We can't go any further today.' He spoke carefully and patiently. The disappointed eyes stimulated his inexplicable affection for the old man. He thought that was what it was.

'Are we any closer?'

The inevitable question. Harper looked at Morag, passing the buck, and received in exchange a non-committal shrug.

'We ought to be,' he said.

Wendover nodded and raised himself on one elbow.

'I think I'll try and walk a bit.'

Harper helped him off the cart, steadying with a hand under his shoulder. The emaciated body weighed nothing. It was trembling with the effort. Harper felt the hard shape of the S & W bang against him.

They stumbled up the sweeping green incline of the cutting, struggling over the rusted remnants of the fence. Morag followed, the cart creaking behind her. Harper reflected wryly that from behind it would be difficult to separate helper from helped: the slope did nothing to favour his twisted leg.

He was teaching Morag to read.

It was hardly more than a gesture on his part, since it turned out that her ability almost equalled his (it stung him) and she needed help only with the more cumbersome constructions. But she had been strangely insistent that he go through the motions. He supposed it was a simplistic attempt to fix their relationship. He was flattered.

Reading together from a thin book, they lay side by side in the shifting orange circle of the firelight, his arm crooked under her head. In the rush to leave, they had taken none of the books from the library: this one, Morag had discovered in the living room of a house in the prolapsed garden suburbs (running to him jubilantly as if it were tinned food, her pinched face lit up, eyes round); it was mystifyingly entitled *Recollections of a Piebald Unicorn, Published by the Vertigone Little Press.*

Wendover and the child were sleeping, the doctor twitching and mumbling in his hot dreams. Arm was a shadowy figure beyond the nifty flames, humming to himself as he made some adjustments to Morag's pack frame. Theoretically, he was on watch. Harper, who was to take the graveyard shift, should have been asleep. He would regret it later in the gritty hours; but it seemed worth sacrificing future comfort to the warmth of the moment. The trees at the ambit of the clearing loomed thick and reassuring; a dark, inscrutable, and deceptively solid escarpment. Somewhere, water was running atonally down to the motorway, where it would disappear into the choked conduits of the cutting.

Most of the text was beyond both of them.

Morag assumed it all meant something to Harper, but he was out of his depth on more occasions than he liked to admit, not even trusting his viscera. It was irritating to attempt for her expansions of half-glimpsed meanings. She read:

> Thalidomide façades in arcs
> the unjointed verticals; the lintel,
> the arch shadowed; crooked
> insurgent sunlight; this tall face
> the emerging city.

It wasn't any city she'd been in, and he was unsure in just what way a thalidomide façade differed from an ordinary one. It was unlikely that Wendover would wake up and supply an answer.

'Well . . .' he said.

Arm relieved him of the difficulty.

The dwarf had clambered to his feet, dropping the frame, and was peering at the far side of the clearing, his back to them and the indistinct lines of his body tense.

Harper let go the book and examined the shoulder of the trees, his eyes confused by the uncertain light. The black wall became hard and uncompromising. He got up, pulling out his gun.

He stepped past the fire, over the prone figure of the doctor, who was speaking rationally in the

alien language of sleep. Arm continued to stare
in front of him.

'Harper?' He seemed nervous. 'Something
moved.'

Harper's eyes slowly grew accustomed to the
gloom. The flickering light behind them made
formless designs on the screen of vegetation.

Silence dragged on until the sound of a twig
snapping just inside the covert became a relief.
The noise was amplified beyond belief by the
night and the uncertainty. Harper jerked back
the slide of the pistol, his hands clammy. Its
double click echoed off the wall of trees. Something impelled him to call: 'Come out, or I'll
shoot . . .'

He was uncomfortably aware of the stupidity
of the challenge, but something came out
anyway.

It slid out of the peripheral foliage with a
fluid, economic motion, and then stood very still,
the firelight fingering dimly across its limbs and
toning them burnt umber.

It was tall and lightly built, a thin, stringy
figure in the gloom. Its total immobility was
unnerving, giving it the air of a life-sized sculp-
ture, which, displaced from its customary artificial surroundings, gains new and undefinable
significances through its juxtaposition with
trees and earth.

Harper shivered, noting the dull, scaly integument: this hide, unlike the child's, was taut, revealing the configuration of the muscles and tendons beneath. The body was naked and hairless, the head a long tapering oval, disproportionately slim. Its eyes reflected, like the eyes of animals. In one bony hand it carried a short spear tipped with a broad spatulate sliver of tin plate.

The tension grew: Harper felt it as a stasis of the air, a suffusion of blood to his neck. Or perhaps that was something else. He kept the gun levelled, but the mutant never moved.

They confronted for long vacuous minutes while Harper dredged his mind for something to say. He noticed that the thing's genitals were encased in some sort of pouch, and wondered if this were in fact part of the integument. He coughed. He said:

'We brought a child . . . Like you, a child . . .'

Dropping the words like stones, one by one, into a hole. They took a long time to fall and did nothing towards alleviating the silence, which closed in after them like a trap. Harper felt a growing sense of futility. The mutant remained quiet, merely watched them from unmoving eyes. Had it understood? He looked for a motion that might indicate its reactions, the twitch of a muscle, a shift in stance. There was none.

'A child,' he repeated, feeling foolish and

apologetic, as if it were his fault that the creature failed to react.

It stood for perhaps five seconds more.

He caught a fleeting, possibly illusory impression of motion: a brief nod, a complex twining of fingers that might have been a reflection of the firelight.

It swung abruptly away and vanished into the covert. The whole dumb show might have been a hallucination. There was a low rustle of disturbed bushes.

Harper let out his breath explosively, left on an unpleasant plateau of frustration. This unilateral try at communication had somehow forced on him the improbable role of failed litigant. The mutant's attitude had compelled him to defend a position he didn't hold. It was not a comfortable way to feel after being driven so far by no other motive than charity.

Arm plainly sensed nothing of the defeat.

'We made it!' he said gleefully, punching Harper's bicep.

'Yes. But I think we might be trespassing. I wonder if the kid's enough?'

'Cheer up,' Arm told him. 'At least we came to the right place.'

He put the pistol away and stared into the fire; threw another piece of wood on to watch the sparks fly about. Anything could be in the spinney.

The Initial Contact

Morag came up to stand beside him, the book hanging from her hand like a dead bird.

'Was it one of them?' And on receiving a curt, self-involved nod: 'They *live* in the woods, you know, and don't wear clothes.' She considered that, stirring the edge of the fire with the toe of her shoe. 'They have quite dirty habits.'

'Don't hold the book like that,' he said. 'You'll break its spine.'

9: The Maps He Had Once Known

Wendover came to the washed-out dawn from a disturbed night. Spectres patrolled his head:

He removed the remaining shards by running the brick round the window-frame, then climbed clumsily in, the Smith & Wesson banging heavily against his hipbone. He was delighted with himself.

Inside, it was shadowy and damp, a small dusty oubliette of a room, grimy blue wallpaper puffing limply where the moisture had got to it. Round-the-wall benches and a pile of rat-chewed pulp on a three-legged table marked it as a waiting room.

He tried the door and entered the passage outside without difficulty. The surgery door was labelled, the rest of the floor blocked by low wooden gates and – customary churlishness – signs saying ABSOLUTELY NO ADMITTANCE TO PATIENTS.

Chrome-appointed desk, shelves and chairs. A

smell of rat droppings, gloom in the corners, and a foetus-shaped stain over the scales. It was dank and dusty and hadn't been disturbed for at least a generation.

He had been poking about for about half an hour — finding a GP's bag, well stocked and superficially in good condition; one or two antiseptic aerosols still pressurized and operating; and the quite impossible luxury of a bottle of whisky — when he heard the turbine again, cruising down the street.

It stopped. A door slammed. The outer door of the surgery rattled.

'Try the window, Arm!' he yelled, involved via a filing cabinet of record cards in an almost pleasant re-creation of the past. The last occupant of the place had apparently been a homoeopath.

There was a pause. He heard a faint noise behind him; turned jubilantly to report his major find; caught a glimpse of a shadowy and unidentifiable figure in the crepuscular light. Then there was an eye-searing burst of flame and a massive pain in his left temple. Echoes hammered round his brain. He fought for reason and attained only a dull feeling of surprise; and it was surely unfair that he had to fight the shadows too. They stirred, leapt out of the corners of the room, and swallowed him up . . .

*

He struggled out of that cold re-enactment to the crying of the child. There was an ache in the small of his back, but his head was for the first time in weeks clear and free from pain. He got up and huddled closer to the wan fire over which Morag was cooking, her hair dark and lank with moisture, her chilled fingers dealing clumsily with the utensils. It was misty. The trees dripped steadily, water filming their limbs with grey light. He sat in silence for some time, blowing into his cupped hands and recalling the events of the early hours. It was a pity to have missed the mutant, but Harper's account of its appearance had catalysed his recovery: he found he could no longer afford illness.

Morag picked up the child, began cleaning it up. It was growing rapidly, filling out its skin. Wendover abandoned his scrutiny of the clearing as a whole and watched the girl, noting the way her face lost its sharp angles as she whispered to the ugly thing. He couldn't make her out. He had grown unused to character judgement. Post-disaster, prediction became impossible, and one was compelled to judge by actions. However, he did sense quite a fine line of distinction between the naive and the amiably stupid: and thinking about it he sensed a danger. He decided to attempt crossing of the bridge in advance.

'We'll be losing him soon,' he said. 'You'll miss him.'

She scraped a strand of hair off her forehead. 'Not all that much,' she answered. 'I've got something instead, haven't I?' Which he could well understand. Her eyes searched the circle of trees. She shook her head. 'You seem better today, Doctor.'

At least she's learned somewhere to avoid the questions she doesn't want to answer, he thought. He hoped she felt no guilt over the transference of affections to Harper. Even if it was complete, would she give up the child with no regrets at all? He didn't like to think that, but he knew he was old-fashioned. At least she had caught up with the zeitgeist.

'There isn't any time for that,' he said. 'After we've done the job there'll be plenty of it. I may relapse then . . .'

Unwittingly, she had touched his own sensitive spot. An eye for an eye, he thought. What *am* I going to do when it's finished? Go back to watching the world fall apart? But I don't have the patience for that any more. So he finished lamely: 'But only if *you* promise to nurse me.'

You silly old man, he thought. She gave him a thin smile, said something secretive to the child, which was dribbling.

With a great deal of noise Harper and Arm emerged from the sullen, damp thicket, carrying

a handful of empty snares each. They had
decided on this method of taking game early on
in the trip, and it had given Wendover a spin-
sterish satisfaction to find that neither of them
possessed his skill in the matter: he thought
that he might have prospered in Tinhouse after
all . . .) Harper picked twigs and burrs from his
hair. The dwarf produced a rabbit from under
his coat, handed it to Morag with the air of a
conjuror waiting for applause.

'There was another,' he said, 'but a fox or
something' – he glanced at Harper – 'got at it
during the night. Then this bugger shoots off his
last bullet to put it out of its misery, and . . .' He
wheezed and doubled up, shaking. He was in a
good mood. 'Pah!' he finished, explosively.

Harper smiled weakly.

'It blew right to pieces,' he said. 'I didn't think
to break its neck.'

'You never think,' Wendover told him.

'Bloody hell!' spluttered Arm: 'A .45 Browning
bullet!'

'I'll be glad to get out of here,' said Harper, to
no one in particular, attempting to change the
subject. 'What do we do? Just sit around waiting
for them to come to us?' He grinned at Wendover
in a most relieved manner. 'Your decision, of
course.'

'I think we'll move on a bit further,' said

Wendover, feeling that he'd missed out on something.

'The whole trespass thing is obsolete. There aren't that many people.'

On the road again.

As they progressed, the woodland backed slowly away from the motorway, leaving in its place low scrub and maquis from which rose isolated thorn saplings. Gorse and briar had grown to great heights, and, weakened by the effort, dropped palely, flecked with the grey of mutated blights. After a mile the forest remained in the middle distance, like a trick of the eye.

'Density makes no difference. And, anyway, these people are . . .' Suffering from aphasia, Harper stumbled over a weed-filled crevice in the metalling, walked on looking sulky.

'You were going to say "primitive"!' crowed Arm. And then, smugly: 'Did I catch just a little suggestion of snobbery there, son?'

'You *know* I didn't . . .'

The fence hung in stiff festoons, beaded with moisture. For as far as they could see, none of its supports had been disturbed; they filed round wide curves, in and out of pools of mist, a caravan of iron veils. It was very quiet. The road curved with them, a simple structural metaphor for Wendover's quest.

'Oh, you may not have *meant* it . . .'

'Drop it, the pair of you,' said Wendover, his patience suffering in the cold air. Even when he had a contribution he didn't like to join in, for fear of encouraging the dreary sparring. 'Arm, stop baiting him.'

Wrecks were more frequent. The corroded shells of fast freighters clogged the freeway, heaps of them rearing up like ancient surrealist battlements. Dwarfed between the flaking hulks, forcing passage, Wendover discerned on scarred flanks fragments of old cellulose, blistered proprietary symbols. Morag hardly said anything at all.

From the hollow, resounding back of a tanker, they surveyed the landscape. They had been walking for perhaps an hour – although it seemed like more – pushing deeper into an extended bank of mist. Visibility was down to thirty yards and shortening. The wrecks wound away south, crawling over one another like frigidly copulating lizards. The steel beneath them was rotting, damp and greasy to the touch, a treacherous footing.

'I suppose it's a waste, really,' murmured Arm, mostly to himself.

He touched Wendover's shoulder.

'Now why should that be, I wonder?'

He pointed vaguely towards the woodland through the mist. Wendover, looking for some particular item rather than a quality of the landscape – and suspecting that, once found, it would prove to be nothing more than a change of subject in the eternal dispute – saw nothing. When he said so, the dwarf shook his head impatiently. 'The bushes, Doctor,' he said.

Wendover examined the scrub.

A wide avenue of broken vegetation had been forced through it, sometime during the preceding two days: the foliage of the flattened saplings and crushed fern hadn't yet dried out. White wood showed at breakages. It ran parallel to the road for some distance, then turned through ninety degrees and vanished into the mist, an enigmatic perspective.

'There haven't been any high winds,' said Arm.

'It would have to be a peculiar wind, anyway, to do that,' offered Harper, with a bright inviting smile.

'Shut *up*,' said Wendover.

Another half-hour's walking brought them to a cloverleaf junction, where the motorway tied itself into a concrete rosette. Sweating grey piers humped it above the mist. Up there, it seemed even colder.

Wendover leaned on a crash barrier and watched the access road trail away like threads from frayed silk. To the east, the last few feet of

a Gothic tower rose above the mist, its crenella-
tions picked out sharply by the bright weak sun.
He tried to remember in which area of the
country they were, but could suggest only
'south', which conjured no associations. Perhaps
they had altogether left the maps he had once
known.

Ostensibly for warmth, Harper and the girl
had huddled together beside the handcart. The
dwarf was stamping his feet and breathing heavily into his cupped hands. Wendover found the
tower more familiar than the customary geog-
raphy of ruined vehicles. It drew him, quite
explicably.

'If nobody minds . . . ?' he said.

They moved off down the incline of the eastern
slip road. Goofing about, Morag and Harper lost
control of the cart, and it rolled down the slope,
faster and faster until it was bound to be upset.

'No I don't *mind*,' said Arm, 'but if you want
my op*in*ion . . .'

The slip road soon turned into a country lane,
degenerate and flanked by ditches full of nettles.
At one time its environs had been predominantly agricultural, neat three- and four-acre
plots of animal feed and root vegetable, but the
break-up had put an end to that.

The vanguard of the forest blurred the edges
of the low-lying fields; young conifers crowded
the remaining patches of sugarbeet and kale

(strains bred for high vendibility, they had not been equipped to compete with less-civilized weeds: but the survivors hung on tenaciously). The thorn hedges had spread, drifting genetically into strange shapes. The mist clung to the undergrowth, anechoic, sucking up the clatter of something that had blackbird in its ancestry, damping the mechanical cawing of the ageless rooks.

Uneasy reveries plagued Wendover: cued by the chilly, tangled landscape, he saw this journey clearly as an act of expiation, the final extension of a line of emotional reasoning made obsolete by the catastrophe.

'Make sure the child is warm enough,' he told Morag. He shivered.

Harper kicked at a rut in the road. He looked up and said: 'Somebody uses this, regularly. Is that a tyreprint?'

Wendover shrugged. 'Ask Arm.'

They drew together. The mist drew round them. Morag tucked the child's swaddlings more firmly. After that it was inevitable that they hear voices.

Infected for a moment by Harper's superstitions, Wendover imagined that they had been followed down the motorway. But noise seemed to be coming from up ahead; individual footsteps merged into an almost rhythmic shuffle, and the voices were an undertone of constant timbre.

'I think we'd better get in the ditch,' advised Arm quietly.

Wendover hesitated, trying to fix direction. A small dog began to bark hysterically. Over the ground bass of feet and voices rose the insistent treble figure of a child repeating some nonsensical litany, a collection of dissociated syllables his mind rendered as:

'What every weevil *knows*, what every *wee*vil *knows*, what *every* weevil kn . . .'

'Down, Doctor,' Arm insisted.

He grasped the skirt of Wendover's coat and dragged him into the nettles. The others dropped in beside him. The bed of the ditch was wet and resilient, smelly and secret beneath chickweed and nightshade. He was stung, but he didn't shout. The nonsense ran on through his head, then stopped abruptly.

An unpleasant congregation wound out of the mist.

It was fronted by two thin men on old, sick horses. The hooves of the animals were muffled in swathes of rag; they stumbled and pecked and drooped their heads listlessly against poor harness. The riders wore tight, dark breeches and carelessly buttoned gaiters, a curiously dated garb. (It took Wendover a little time to realize that it was the whole concept of uniformity that was dated. He felt absurdly pleased, as if another brick had been added to the structure of his own personal disaster: he had the new world that much more under his thumb.) Each carried a wooden staff. Their faces were lean and sombre, cancered, similar and stupid, and they rode with uncomfortably curved spines.

Behind them, in groups of four and five, filed what seemed to be the entire complement of a village.

Pinched children in old overcoats and windcheaters followed the horses closely with leather buckets, hoping for dung. Sporadically, one or another of them would chant the first few syllables of the absurd litany, then cease and look guiltily about. Their parents were segregated: the women carried or dragged toddlers and stared ahead at the children; the men came on with a faintly militaristic gait, staffs over their shoulders. Some of them had charge of small, noisy dogs on multiple leads.

They exuded the same tangible ectoplasm of poverty and hopelessness as the inhabitants of Tinhouse, the same air of patient acceptance: but added to this was a strange repressed exultation. Wendover sensed that it was linked to the threadbare, voluminous clothes, bleached out and drab, the mixture of almost formal silence and dull talk in a broad southern accent.

He had met it before, but could not remember the circumstances.

The aged were unsegregated: they trailed the end of the progression, strung out and stumbling as often as the horses, men and women both, their expressions pained or vacant. As they dawdled past, Morag changed her position uneasily. Harper put his fingers to his lips, nudged her.

The child, thrust into the nettles as she shifted about to keep her balance, let out a short preliminary cry, then began to scream.

Immediately, the procession broke into confusion: an ancient shrivelled woman in a calf-length print dress shrieked at her neighbours; younger men milled back among the sexagenarians, complaining in loud, sullen voices; an old man stopped to wet himself, staring blankly into the distance like a stalling animal. One of the horses came trotting back, throwing a spavined foreleg grotesquely to the left at each step.

The old woman grabbed its owner's stirrup, gesticulated, and waved violently towards the ditch. Her stringy jowls shook with indignation. He shook his head. She tugged at his leg. More concerned to get rid of her than to investigate, he flailed the horse forward with his heels. She fell down, and he ignored her.

"Ere! They got a *frog* down there!' he shouted, looking directly down at Wendover in the ditch.

He dropped his reins, swung his staff in a terrible arc. Wendover ducked, but it caught his shoulder a nasty blow. He fell to his hands and knees, sank to his wrists in the muck.

'Come on out,' yelled the horseman. 'Come out!'

The rest of the procession surged to the edge of the ditch. Some of the aged, their faces turned abruptly malicious – eyes protruding, wattles a-tremble – were pushed in inadvertently. Arm broke an old man's nose with his gnarly fist, provoking a spate of blood quite remarkable for someone in such a desiccated condition. Harper swore.

Eventually they were dragged out and manhandled into the centre of the road, where they stood in a huddle, Arm and Harper looked surly, Morag placating the offended child.

'We'll 'ave that,' said the horseman, pointing at Morag. Two women and a man came forward from the bucolic crew around him and made to take the baby. Harper stood in the way.

'Piss off,' he said, snatching the man's staff. The women spat at him, and he laid the stick about their necks. The man kicked his bad knee from behind; drove an elbow into his kidneys; took the weapon back and clubbed him down with it.

Arm shuffled forward, his fingers hooked, his stance canny and murderous.

'No, Arm,' said Wendover. He felt very weary and hardly knew what to do. Plainly, there wasn't much to be gained by making a stand. The dwarf shot him a look of anger, then shrugged. Wendover turned to the horseman.

'What is it you want from us?'

He had remembered his gun, but couldn't make up his mind to use it.

'Oh, don't you play dumb with *us*,' the man replied, giving his reins a vigorous shake. His horse chewed at its nickel bit with tough, rubbery lips. There were patches of black skin on its neck where the reins had rubbed the hair off. Perversely, Wendover's mind threw up images of other horses in other times, a simple adamant statement of nostalgia. 'You know what *we* want all right. And don't we know it!' He smiled slyly about to demonstrate his logic.

Harper groaned and got to his feet, leaning heavily on the dwarf, who was massaging his back for him. Morag was fighting a silent tug of war for the child, plucking grimly at the flat beastly faces of the women.

Wendover ran a hand over his face, thinking, I'm far too old.

When he looked at the scene again it had frozen into a tableau. Arm was gazing into the mist, a musing cast to his features, his head tilted.

A deep mechanical moan swelled up from the

verge of audibility. Hearing it, the horses stamped their feet, and the eyes of the horsemen shifted nervously about. The rest of the villagers stared in the direction from which they had come. Arm grinned suddenly and said something in a low voice to Harper.

10: The Floating Nun

The sound mounted in volume, modulated perceptibly to a high and steady scream that scraped the inner ear. Soon, the mist became violently agitated, billowing down to ground level in pale vortices and then shooting up again to spread out like steam twenty-five or thirty feet up. The effect was harassing.

Wendover performed another act of mental submission. He had come to dislike himself intensely for these continual cop-outs. He tried to argue that they were circuit breakers. He had made the same point for several years when living with Vanessa: it had been a casuistry then, too, and now he found himself unable to remember her face.

A big LWN hovercraft hunched slowly out of the mist. Its snout was blunt, leprous and peeling, occupying the whole width of the road. Its slanted cockpit windows caught the grey, diffuse

light, giving it a saurian personality: blind and
inexorable.

'Ah-*ha*,' said Arm, with a gleam in his eye.

Ears back, the horses circled nervously, tread-
ing on each other's hooves and tearing off strips
of the muffling. For easier handling, both men
had dismounted, delegated their staffs, and
taken the animals on a short rein beneath the
bit.

'Wait yer sweat, Dora Meadows,' muttered one
of them, jerking at the beast's mouth and eyeing
the hover warily. The horse rubbed against his
shoulder, easing a weeping sore beneath its eye.

'Sister'll sort *this* one out,' he told his compan-
ion, 'don't you worry about *that*.' He indicated
Morag with a sober nod. 'Them bloody tight
trousers, eh?' he said. 'Eh? It makes you wonder
with trousers like that.'

The LWN came to a halt ten yards off, swinging broadside on to them, howling and sucking
up mist. On its shabby flank was a flaking
caption, TRUNK RAT S. It sank slowly on its
rubber skirt with a sigh audible above the
diminishing sound of the lift engine. Settled, it
straddled the road and both ditches.

'Hah,' said Arm. 'He'll regret that. The jet's
not peaking. They never service the stuff.' This
latter with a fine contempt, showing his nasty
teeth.

The hatch above and behind the cockpit fell

back against the roof with a metally clatter. A hand reached up from inside, clutched the coaming and pulled into view an ambiguously sexed figure dressed in a long, loose grey robe, a tight white hood, and what seemed to be a veil. It began to descend the ladder attached to the side of the vehicle, hampered by its skirts and moving laboriously.

So they never quite died out, thought Wendover.

The figure got closer, focussed sexually: a woman about as old as himself. A big bosom, in no way suggestive of breasts; a short, determined stride; the face blurred behind the veil. He wondered if she was cancered. Presumably she would wear the veil regardless, but there had been a big influx in the calling shortly after the symptoms had begun: a shock to the authorities after the recruit shortage and nun-running of the early seventies.

Her hands were large, the veins standing well up from the skin.

'I'm Sister Dooley,' she said, assessing him as locus of the group. Her voice came as no surprise, capable, too loud. 'Now. You're not people of mine, are you? No. You're welcome anyway, of course.'

What a bloody attitude. He nodded curtly. He was tired, and sick of people who couldn't face facts.

'Now. What's going on, Mr Meadows?'

Meadows led his Dora forward, jerking at her mouth when she tried to crop the grass verge. He touched his forelock.

'They got a frog, Sister. Won't give it up, neither,' he grumbled. He shoved the mare's face away as it muzzled his neck. He pointed a finger at Morag. 'There.'

The nun peered through her veil. Take the bloody thing off and stop messing about, thought Wendover.

She went and stood in front of Morag, looked her up and down for a moment, and said: 'Goodness me, child. Have you no clothes to wear? Do answer me now.'

Morag set her face and whispered to the baby. Harper limped up with Arm at his side.

'Leave the kid alone,' he said. He never gave up.

Sister Dooley studied him. 'I had no thought of touching it at all.'

She came back to Wendover and Meadows, who had been covertly scrutinizing one another in the stiff truce. Wendover was quite sure of his position regarding the nun's priest. He caught himself thinking like a silly old man: When *I* have a stick.

'You should not have tried to take it from her, Mr Meadows.'

And to Wendover:

'It was a mistake on his part. The child is her responsibility for a little while, you would say that?'

Wendover started, taken unawares by the accuracy of the prediction. He opened his mouth to reply, but she cut in, 'then I'm sure you'll allow me to arrange the necessary when it comes?'

He could hardly believe their luck. Christ, he thought, she's got contact with the main body. We're home and dry.

'I'd like to see it through, of course,' he said, 'but I'll be glad to hand over to you eventually. You've had experience with the mutants? We found it hard to communicate.'

'Oh yes, that *was* the old name. Yes, I know them. I've become quite adroit, in fact. There are so many of them here. I've been doing my imperfect best to ease the situation locally for almost ten years now.'

He thought he might get to like her despite the cant. Obviously she lived in a vanished past, but he should have expected charity, if nothing else. Whether he would allow her to take his final responsibility he didn't know. He offered her his hand. When she didn't react, he smiled instead. She had forgotten more than he had, which pleased him obscurely.

'I'm Wendover,' he said.

'Yes. Now, if you and your people will follow me . . .'

She strode back to the hover. Meadows walked with her a few steps, but was forced to fall back when his mare refused to approach the machine.

'Giddiap, eh? Eh?' Wendover said to him, carefully skirting the snorting animal.

The bulkhead dividing the LWN's cockpit from the cargo bay had been knocked crudely out, and the remaining ragged edges of pressed steel hammered flat against the sides and roof. The bay was about thirty feet by eleven, and had been used to house or transport animals: although it had recently been scrubbed, a sour smell of ammonia hung in the air. There were tethering rings spaced along one wall.

The cockpit was laid out with dual controls and a long bench seat. Its only complication was a bank of pressure gauges above the windscreen, but several of these had been simplified radically and hung loose and rusty from their sockets. It was a dim place.

Arm went immediately to examine the equipment while the others stood wrinkling their noses in the cargo space, waiting for the nun. Outside, Meadows had relinquished the mare to one of his subordinates and was craning his neck up to talk to her as she leaned out of the open hatch. Wendover noticed that the rest of the villagers had collected into a quiet, disciplined body some distance away from the LWN and were looking on respectfully, hats in gullible hands.

'You'll take the villagers and begin the thing properly, you're sure you remember now. Hurry them up now, we've lost a lot of the morning here.' She came down the internal steps and saw Arm.

'Stand away from there, young man. It's a difficult enough job to keep the machine running at all. I'm no mechanic.'

'I see,' said Arm. Then, with polite cheer: 'Well, it won't be running much longer, will it? Your injectors are shot, and there may not be enough instrumentation left to adjust them. It's walking you'll have to be, and fairly soon.'

In frigid silence Sister Dooley settled herself in her seat, sinking slowly on to her skirts with considerable patience.

'I'm forty-odd, actually,' said Arm.

The LWN lifted unevenly, yawed: for a moment it was driving sideways, and Wendover saw a plunging horse reel past the blunt bow, lashing out with lumpy hooves. Sister Dooley turned it immediately off the road, ploughed through the hedge, and began to travel due east at speed.

She handled the machine with an odd combination of caution and negligence, carefully avoiding one clump of vegetation, then meeting a perfectly similar one with enough impetus to uproot it, cutting a broad swathe of destruction. Wendover clung to the back of the seat, lacking the courage to sit in the unoccupied half. Next to him, Arm stared fixedly ahead with the stunned expression of a rabbit eyeing a ferret.

The decayed agriculture gave way to trees, which the nun was forced to detour. Wendover's 'forest' was revealed as a five-hundred-yard frieze of fir and elm, superseded in its turn by flat, marshy ground cut with muddy streams. Covens of rooks fled meetings in the elms, tumbling unhappily into the air.

Through clouds of spray the damp landscape lurched violently. The noise was incredible. Wendover calculated from the shivering needle of the ASI that they had already travelled further than he had walked that morning. If the Sister kept pace, the villagers had no hope of catching up.

The hover sideswiped the solid bole of a willow and ricocheted on to a broad, slow waterway. Wildfowl panicked up in flocks from an acre of sere reed-beds.

'East?' Arm yelled into Wendover's ear, but it didn't mean anything to him until a few minutes later when the waterway broadened into an estuary lined with rotting pleasure boats, and he caught a glimpse of the sea, a smoky horizon.

Morag cried out briefly, smiling and pointing.

Sister Dooley put on more speed, barrelling past midstream eyots and scuppered fishing smacks. The engine noise batted back unheard from the wreckage of a small port. She swung the craft through ninety degrees to parallel the coast, heading north in the shallows just off a shingle beach.

Arm shrugged, shook his head in puzzlement.

It was now impossible to turn inland: to the left above the tideline rose the dark backs of marram-anchored artificial dunes, built to prevent erosion, rising to eighty and a hundred feet above sea-level. And out of the choppy sea to starboard rose the abandoned off-shore drilling rigs, some of them listing on broken stilts.

Sister Dooley exclaimed petulantly; throttled back, wrenched the hover to port. The dunes bulked enormously in the windscreen, an imminent disaster. Wendover hung on hard, predicting a wreck. Was the woman mad?

At the terminal instant, great dun shoulders flashed past right and left as the LWN shot the gap left in the earthworks for another mouth of the river. The sea diminished as Sister Dooley throttled up and headed inland again.

After ten minutes travelling back along their original course, she put the thrust jet into reverse and stopped the vehicle on a patch of bare fenland fringed with low scrub, willow and elder. They were very near their point of departure. The motorway would be off somewhere to the right. A last few wisps of mist idled over the fen, which was black and loamy where the reeds didn't grow. A heron on a rotting stump regarded them morosely.

'Well!' said the nun.

Wendover could make nothing of the silly journey. He drew in breath, to say so.

'Hush now,' she said.

In the silence, his ears throbbed. Vague shufflings and breathings became noticeable. The frame of the hover popped and creaked. A lot of shouting began in the vegetation ahead.

'I get behind them, you see,' she said, 'and then they're between us.'

The villagers came on through the scrub, spread out along a four-hundred-yard arc, heading direct for the LWN. The women and children were caterwauling and making a din by beating on buckets and tins. The men were flailing the undergrowth with their staves, beating to a rhythm called by the two horsemen. Meadows, at the left-hand end of the line, cupped his hands round his mouth and shouted at his opposite number. The arc closed up, became a funnel opening out on to the fen. There was a commotion at the edge of the scrub.

Three full-grown mutants scattered on to the fen, running with difficulty on the boggy surface, their long strange heads swinging hurriedly in an attempt to assess the nature of the pursuit. Their scaly hides were daubed with mud. They saw the hover and stopped so suddenly that one of them fell and dropped his spear.

Caught between the racket of the beaters and the wail of Sister Dooley's turbine, they hesitated, confused.

'You *bastard!*' screamed Harper at the nun, because he had lived long enough with Holloway Pauce to make the relevant associations.

She ignored him and dragged the throttle back. The LWN shot forward, throwing him into a heap on the floor with Morag and the child. Wendover grabbed at the seat, missed, went sprawling. Acceleration pinned him down. He thought, Christ, Christ.

He struggled up. He could do nothing but watch.

The villagers caught their quarry easily, engulfing them. But there was a scuffle, some kicking and punching, and one of the mutants broke away suddenly. He avoided Meadows and his mare and ran off at great speed, twisting and dodging and roaring in an unknown language.

Sister Dooley clucked and went after him with the hover, matching every leap and twist with the cumbersome blunt thing, her splendidly capable hands firm on the steering column. She followed his deep footprints and ran him ragged to the brink of a stream. He lay there and panted, his flexible tongue quivering.

The hover was almost touching him, its airstream spattering him with fibrous black ooze and agitating the surface of the water behind him. He waited trembling until Meadows and some footmen came to take him.

With the stabilizing of the hover's deck, Harper got to his feet. His nose was bleeding. Somebody was rattling the rear hatch of the cargo bay. It dropped away with a crash and became a loading ramp. Light surged into the bay. Wendover put a hand on the cripple's shoulder. He shook it off.

'Whoever you are,' he said to the nun's back, 'you deserve to be killed.'

He made a fist. She had been watching his reflection in the windscreen. She reached quickly under the seat and turned round with a machine pistol. It was too late for any shooting on Wendover's part.

'It seems I have been mistaken with you, being heathens from somewhere in the north as you are. It is a pity that things have got to such a pitch all over the place that I have no help at all from you in this. You deceived me, and I am an old woman.'

The villagers were crowding into the hover, children and all. They had fastened rope halters very tightly about the necks of the mutants, and proceeded to tether them, pulling the ropes right through the rings until each victim's head was forced hard against the wall. They laughed and nudged each other's rib. A few of them held up their children so that they could poke sticks.

'Me next, me!' shouted the children.

'Mr Meadows,' said the nun, motioning him from the press, 'there is trouble here now. Somebody will take your good horse back to the village while you keep your eye well fixed on these here to see they do not move.'

She gave him the machine gun, which he handled gingerly.

'Stand over there,' she told Wendover. 'It's uncivilized that you should force me to do such things to smooth-skinned people, but I'll have you tethered if I must. Perhaps Mr Meadows can persuade you back to the reason of the Lord while I drive us.'

'Fuck the Lord,' said Arm, indistinctly.

The villagers backed out of the hover and slammed the loading hatch into place.

'With a broom,' said Arm.

On the journey back, Wendover began the slow, attritive processes of conscience. It would have been so simple to deduce Sister Dooley's position from her earlier conversation had he not been prepared to hear what he needed to hear. Even the promptings of his own prejudice had been a defence mechanism, but he had relaxed and run with events, thinking like a peasant.

He wondered if the illness was at the root of his consistent lack of discrimination: but that was another cop-out – his inability to resolve his problems with Tinhouse or to manage the group successfully had already symptomized muddy thinking. And the sense of relief, now quite vanished away ... Of course, he was being unfair to himself.

Mr Meadows converted them to no reason of any kind, because he did not speak. He regarded them with hostility and suspicion (less, on the whole, than he reserved for the machine pistol, which was an early-model Tonge-Bennetto running on three magazines taped together and having a fur of corrosion on its external parts) and looked occasionally with disgust at the mutants.

Harper stared angrily at the broad shoulders of the nun, licking the blood off his top lip and twice abandoning the idea of attacking Meadows; Morag huddled over the child, exhorting it to silence; and Arm had his head cocked, as if listening – at one point, he nodded insinuatingly at Wendover, as if conveying information of some import.

Sister Dooley gave them a comparatively smooth ride. She didn't want Mr Meadows to lose his balance.

The mutants gazed patiently in whatever direction their individual bonds allowed. They did not attempt to talk. Their skin gave off a pleasant, faint musk, but one of them had urinated down himself, possible through fear. They did not seem to have noticed the child and for its own part it kept up a grey complaint.

11: The Bridge at Evening

Wendover's teeth were aching again. It might have been guilt, or something in the vibration of the hovercraft: shortly before they had regained the road, its drive jet had begun to run rough, fading intermittently until Sister Dooley could make little more than steerage way under full throttle. The LWN drifted along at walking pace, yawing aimlessly like a water bird on a quiet current. The tower Wendover had noticed from the motorway came into view, its earlier attraction revealed as an unwitting betrayal which he added to his catalogue of foolishness.

The LWN guttered and stopped. It continued to hover, but there was no more impulsion. Sister Dooley wedged the throttle open and hammered at its housing with the heel of her hand.

'Isn't that a thing, Mr Meadows, and so near too?'

Meadows glanced superstitiously into the cockpit section and looked quickly away again, nodding. Wendover rubbed his painful jaw and marked how the shadow of an elm fell across the tranquil fawn stone of the tower; the other trees prevented him from discovering the nature of the rest of the building; and if there were a village ahead, he couldn't see it. It was about noon, and the villagers were still a long way behind.

Arm's expression had become smug. He said to Sister Dooley: 'I might do something.'

He waved a hand at Meadows and the machine gun, politely raised his burnt out eyebrows. He looked a sight in his charred clothes. She peered at him.

'Let him come forward, Mr Meadows, though why he should put himself out in this way . . .'

'Just think of it as a penitence, Sister. If I could have a look at your gear . . . ?'

'What would you know about it, now?'

'You get a bit of water in your paraffin (you couldn't help that even in the old days), and fungus grows in it. No, honestly. It blocks the injectors and all, now.'

It sounded a bit strange to Wendover.

'How would I know I'm not to be gulled by all this?'

Arm snapped his fingers.

'Because you can shoot me.'

That bore no close examination. Wendover imagined small porcine eyes behind the veil, impaling Arm as an insurance against deception. He wished the dwarf would stop goading her with the fake Irish accent. What was he after, anyway?

It was a surprise when she said, 'Very well. Show me.'

Arm stood on the seat under her close scrutiny and joined a corroded wire to one of the loose pressure guages. He tapped it smartly, and a little needle peaked then dropped back again to fibrillate rapidly against its stop.

'See?' he said. He closed the throttle, switched off the drive turbine. She followed his actions intently, her breath whiffling against the veil. It limited his elbow room.

'Now,' he said. 'we blow them clear. Of course, it's a short-term measure.' He did something that started a pump beneath the deck. There was a faint sizzling sound. A smell of hot kerosene filled the cabin. He let the operation continue for some seconds, and throughout it the lift jet kept up a steady moan. He'll blow us up, thought Wendover.

Withdrawing his hand, Arm brushed it accidentally against the dead throttle lever. Sister Dooley hissed. He shut it down ostentatiously.

'And you'll want it trimmed to the new power load.' He fiddled with a calibrated knob. 'There.' It all sounded very authentic.

'Stand away now. Should it work, you'll have my thanks.'

'Don't thank me, thank the Lord.'

She went carefully over the controls, touching everything he had altered in identical order of priority. Then she restarted the drive jet. It idled with a new note. She opened the throttle circumspectly.

The hover lunged forward.

Wendover braced himself.

Morag went down, twisting to fall under the child.

There was a tremendous groan from somewhere under the engine cowlings. It rose to a shriek. The machine gun went *bok* once, and jammed. The lift jet failed. The hover hit the road still accelerating savagely.

Sister Dooley banged her head against the windscreen, slumped. Harper leapt on Meadows and began inexpertly to strangle him. Paraffin ran over the deck. Arm took the machine pistol and jacked a dented shell out of the breech. Some shouting began outside, but a fair way off.

Wendover dragged himself up the steps, barking his shins in haste, and burst the hatch open.

'Trim!' cried Arm. 'Oh, you *stupid* bitch!'

He giggled and shuffled his feet in an awkward little dance.

Harper helped Morag up. He caught Arm's

attention and pointed to the mutants, who had suffered most from the speed seesaw. They hung from the tethering rings by their hands, easing the nooses, necks rubbed raw. 'What about these?'

'No time, forget them,' the dwarf told him, swarming up the ladder.

Agreeing, but privately repelled by Arm's callousness, Wendover nodded to add emphasis. 'We'll have to go, Harper.' He took out his S & W, settled his duffel-bag more firmly, and jumped off the roof.

Landing, he hit his chin on his knees, sending a wave of agony through his rotting jaw. The villagers were approaching in a ragged line from the opposite side of the vehicle. He fired into them; then, with the dwarf beside him, stumbled into the ditch and forced his way through the overgrown hedge.

'Where's Harper?'

'Oh, Christ!'

They wriggled back through the blackthorn. There was a flat report. A bullet whipped past Wendover's head.

Sister Dooley was standing in the hatchway, aiming the second barrel of a shotgun adapted to fire solid slugs. Her veil was up, but the distance was too great to divine her features. Villagers were milling round the LWN. Arm let off the machine pistol, but it threw visibly to the left, and he missed.

Sister Dooley loaded up and drove them through the hedge for the last time.

'The bugger stayed behind. I told him to leave them . . .'

'We'll go back and fetch him.'

'You're as stupid as he is. Come *on*!' Bullets tore through the hedge. It shook to its roots as some of the villagers shoved through.

Wendover was horrified. 'We can't leave them . . .' But he found himself running through the scrub, sweating.

Arm got down on one knee behind some gorse and expended a couple more rounds above the heads of the villagers.

'Later, you hear me?' he said vehemently, breaking his fingernails in an attempt to elevate the rusty backsight of the gun.

'Get into those trees. We're splitting up. You meet me on the road, up on the clover-leaf after dark.' He finished with the sight, tried it out. He had to switch magazines. 'Bloody Home Guard stuff. Until then, hide. Don't go near the hover or the village. Understand?'

Wendover nodded his head miserably.

'Right. I've got the trick of this thing. Get a shift on and I'll cover you. Dawdle and you're on your own.'

He killed three of the villagers in the time it

took Wendover to reach the trees. He was an expert. They retreated without the bodies.

Wendover made the conifers and ran sobbing through them, tripping over roots and ground ivy. Once, he dropped his pistol, and it went off with a huge noise. He lost his medical kit.

With that, he sensed he had initiated a whole new phase.

He skulked among the wrecks for several hours, changing his hiding place several times. He bit his split lips and suffered shooting pains in his upper gums. No one had followed him. After reloading the revolver, he found only a few cartridges left in his pocket. One of them was rimless, and didn't fit the gun. He constructed delusive plans for the rescue of the rest of the group. The panic receded slowly and left him with something else: there had been a shift of emphasis, and he felt that it might have been triggered during his illness by Arm's predilection for violence.

The motorway was quiet, stretching into the past, both north and south.

By evening, he was morose, although quite sure the dwarf would make it. He stood on the complex anagram of the cloverleaf, brooding over an immense white expanse of mist, into which vanished the vague supporting piers beneath him. He blew on his fingers, walked up and down waiting for the moon. He felt cold and vacant. The mist had risen at sunset, cutting short all his internal disputes and reaffirming his dependence on Arm's distasteful capabilities. A temperature inversion at chest height kept it low and eerie. The access roads emerged from it like ramps from an alien sea, and there were wrecked vehicles in the shallows.

The moon came up bright and a day off full. Re-broadcast by the mist, its light revealed considerable detail and gave him a shadow. Boredom impelled him to pay attention to his surroundings, and he couldn't put down memories. There were no clouds.

Arm came up the slip road from the village, whistling. He rose from the sea in stages as the ramp inclined, growing tall in an ectoplasmic way: a disconnected torso, hips, then long legs. He paused beneath the doctor on the ascending access spiral, leant on the low crash barrier and looked down at the mist. He fumbled with his clothing and relieved himself out into space, then moved unhurriedly up the slope. Its final curve obscured him, brought him to Wendover's level. When he reappeared he was extremely close, still whistling, and a total stranger.

Wendover inhaled hard, chilling his painful mouth. He aimed the pistol from the pocket of the raincoat.

The man was tall and ectomorphic. He wore

bright blue trousers, a white shirt with lace ruffles at the collar and cuffs, and a bottle-green jacket washed out towards beige by the moonlight. All the colours were unproven theories.

Heavy rings glittered on his fingers and his long face seemed to be entirely devoid of cancers. His shoulder-length black hair was tied back with a white ribbon. He had a wispy little beard. His feet were bare. His tune had three notes.

Across his back he carried a dark bundle.

He stopped whistling when he saw Wendover. He smiled.

'Now here's a boost,' he said, in a voice curiously devoid of accent.

He made no sudden moves.

'You wouldn't have a match, I suppose?'

Nonplussed, Wendover let go the Smith & Wesson.

'No – I – I lost my bag.'

'Ah.'

He looked disappointed.

He put down his bundle, leaned companionably on the parapet at Wendover's elbow and stared up at the moon. He didn't seem to be too cold in his thin jacket. He whistled a bit more of the monotonous tune. After a while he said:

'Well, it's a sod of a thing, isn't it?'

He picked up his bundle, adjusted a leather strap, shrugged it across his shoulders. His expression was bland, unreadable. He smiled.

He walked off in a northerly direction and waded back into the sea, his deceptive strides taking in large amounts of ground. He vanished among the wrecks.

An hour later the real Arm arrived, his weapon at a jaunty angle. His face and hands were filthy. There was a restrained air of energy about him. Wendover, his nerves raw and jumpy, reached for his pistol even though he'd identified the dwarf. A hand closed tightly on his wrist.

'Steady on,' said Arm. 'No trouble?'

'No,' said Wendover, feeling foolish, 'not really.'

The dwarf released his arm and looked round. 'Pretty exposed up here. Not that it matters much, I suppose.' He aimed the machine gun at the north-bound freeway. 'What we need to find is a truck I noticed down there this morning. I don't know exactly where it is.'

He set out at a stiff pace.

Wendover caught up and asked, 'What's happening?' His own voice surprised him, weak and peevish.

'Ah-ha. I went to the village and snided about. They're all right still. She's got them in a church.' He hawked histrionically, and spat.

'Why did you tell me to keep away?' accused Wendover, but he was more relieved than wounded. Arm looked up at him with an expression of surprise grossly exaggerated by his blacked-up face, eyeballs round and white.

'But you'd have blown it. Creeping around isn't a good thing at your time of life, let's face it.'

'You're getting smug.'

'It was a joke. Hard shit, if that's your attitude. I get the job done.'

He went silent and set himself to the examination of a burnt-out refrigerator rig. When Wendover asked, 'What are we going to do now?' he pretended not to hear. Wendover repeated it.

'We're going to get them out. Unless you've any other orders, Dr Wendover.'

Wendover didn't want to apologize, feeling he had been forced into the wrong role.

'I'm sorry, Arm,' he said.

The dwarf laughed, but he wasn't quite mollified. 'You're a pisser,' he said.

'You know,' he went on suddenly, 'I'm forty-six years old. You wouldn't credit it, would you? I could be a godsend to any village, but they'd treat me like a wet-rag, too.'

There was nothing to say to that. Arm's personal catastrophe had been birth. He went nowhere towards solving his own problems, neither was it to be expected of him. Aware of old advisory failures in remote consulting rooms,

Wendover thought that trying to help would be no help at all.

They came to a light transporter that had been damaged only by time. It had been abandoned late in the disaster period, and its rear doors were still locked. Levering with a long steel bar, they broke it open.

Inside were stacked small-quantity chemical orders for some dead minor business. It was a dangerous load. Arm sorted through the straw-packed crates, lifting them carefully out on to the tailboard for examination in the moonlight. He splintered one of them and took out a small packet.

'Put that away until I ask for it.'

He went back into the wagon and found a two-gallon container labelled SEVENTY PER CENT SOLUTION H_2O_2 WITH CARE. He smiled reminiscently.

'Hold that,' he told the doctor, 'while I go and get some other things. Don't drop it.'

Wendover accepted the canister gingerly, sat moodily on the bed of the wagon. The dwarf scrabbled mysteriously about among nearby bits of wreckage. He picked things up and threw them down again. 'No,' he said, and 'Sod it.' He prised the door of the transporter off its hinges. He came back with an empty quart bottle, a brass nut, a large unopened can of lubricating oil, and a bit of neoprene tubing.

'Go away,' he said. 'It's a bugger if you make a mistake.'

Wendover shook his head and stayed where he was.

'Bah,' said Arm.

He removed the heavy lead seal of the peroxide container and poured one and a half pints of it into the bottle. He tore strips from his trouser legs, rolled some of them into a tight ball and wedged them into the neck of the bottle above the fluid. He hissed anxiously between his teeth.

He forced the filler-cap off the fuel tank of the transporter, and pushed his piece of tubing inside. He opened the oil can and poured most of it on the ground. Then he sucked the end of the tube, spluttered and gagged, and when a nice stream of fuel was soaking into the road, filled the oil can with it.

'Just enough oil left in there,' he muttered to himself.

The remaining strips of cloth he used to seal the oil can. He felt in his pocket.

'Will you look at *that*,' he said, reverently. It was a large spool of multi-cored soldering wire.

'Worth a bloody fortune. What a pity.'

He used it to bind the bottle tightly to the oil can. He held up the brass nut.

'That doesn't go in till later, eh?' He seemed to find that funny. He put it in his pocket. 'Right. Remind me to carry the thing the right way up.'

Wendover, to whom none of this meant a thing, said: 'Will it work, whatever it is?' He had the feeling that he should have been more congratulatory.

'Mm. It should. We'd better get a move on. They're having some sort of meeting pretty soon. A *mass*, I suppose. You'd better have the machine-gun. They still turn to Jesus in their times of trouble.'

He held the odd device to his chest as they went. After a difficult patch of scrambling over the choked wrecks, he fell behind. When Wendover looked back, all he could see was a dark bullet head, bobbing independently above the white mist.

Morag: in the afternoon Sister Dooley had supervised her firmly into a generous grey felt dress and woollen knickers that itched. It was civilized, she explained and a penance. Harper's dogged resistance had collapsed after threats to the child. Now, shepherded from the cottage in which they had been shut all afternoon and brought to a stone place, Morag was unable to relate.

It was draughty, high-ceilinged, dimly lit with candles made from animal fat, which sputtered and stank. The pews had been torn out for firewood during some hard January. The east window was an arched hole framed by jagged shards of coloured glass. The villagers were lined up in rows, holding their hats. Under the empty window was Sister Dooley, assisted by Meadows with his long knife.

At least Arm and the old man had got away.

Soon it would be her turn. She had managed to keep the child quiet, but something would happen to it sooner or later, and she would never see it again. She hugged it, gazing at the thick pillars that supported the ceiling, watching villagers shuffle up the nave between them. They filed in an orderly fashion past Sister Dooley, reforming the rows when she had finished them.

Soon it would be her turn. Everybody got a little cube of raw meat and a drink from Sister Dooley's cup. There had been some singing. The dead mutant lay to one side, its innards revealed. They had tied up the other two in an outhouse because they only needed one at a time for the Celebration. The eating and drinking, which Sister Dooley had promised to explain to her afterwards, was carried out in silence.

She looked down at Harper, where he was crouched heaving emptily on the floor.

Soon after the meeting had begun and Meadows had finished with the mutant, he had thrown up most of his food and tried to attack the nun. He was whimpering with pain and frustration. She wanted to touch him, but there was a strong woman at her shoulder. It was

strange not to have found any reference to True
Love in the books he liked.

Soon she would have to have a drink, too.

At the back of the place, somebody opened the
door and made the draught worse. She knew she
would faint or be sick.

12: The Celebration

The boot had struck just above his genitals. He made a great effort to straighten himself against the cramp in his lower belly.

A dull, unbearable anger diminished his pain. Where were Arm and Wendover now with their pragmatic guns? A tremor shook him. To see her face collapse under the veil, the jaw unhinged, spittle and blood. In this way, he fuelled himself, unaware that he had been born into a common currency, that he merely reflected the slaughter of the mutant. He got himself up on one knee by filling his head with obscenity.

Upright against the wall, palms flat on the gritty damp stone. Immediately there was a villager in front of him, his eyes blank, his staff a warning.

Morag looked like a peasant in her peasant clothes. Her placidity was a feeble defence mechanism. He could do nothing for her. He experienced a surge of loathing for himself and everybody else. The world was psychotic and tasted of bile. There were still nine or ten communicants to be served under the window, and in the dim, guttery light their faces were rapt.

He found that hardest of all to understand: to feel ecstasy though bestiality might be simple – to achieve a similar state from the rationalization of one's own bestiality was something else. He presumed that Holloway Pauce must have felt something similar.

Smoke from the candles had gathered in a dark pall under the roof. As the west door opened, air currents shredded and dispersed it. The candles flickered, shifting the perspective of the nave, distorting the angle of a shoulder here, the set of a head there.

Sister Dooley lifted the cup, tilted it, lifted, tilted, glancing at nervous shadows that played on the tombs and windows of the transepts.

There was a skitter of motion by the font. A draught caught the door and slammed it back against its stop, where it banged to and fro, alternately compressing and expanding a trapezium of grey moonlight. The shadows capered and twisted their limbs.

Morag had joined the file of communicants.

A small fizzing object described a quick flat trajectory over the heads of the congregation and landed with a faint patter in front of the nun. Meadows stepped towards it. Sister Dooley dropped the cup, spilling glutinous fluid down the chest of the communicant. The vessel pealed musically on the stone floor.

Sister Dooley turned her back on the celebrants, reached for something.

Meadows was blinded at the same moment as Harper when the missile flared into a globe of bitter light.

Footsteps rang down the nave.

A harsh, hollow voice cried: 'Harper! Harper! Harper! Harper!'

It might have been in his own head.

Sister Dooley's shotgun boomed, echoes racketing round the pillars. Somebody screamed. Harper's first attempt to move bruised his cheek against a wall, which was hidden behind a tremulous purple haze. A hand fastened on his arm. He lashed out, struck the wall.

'Steady,' said Arm.

An automatic weapon started up from somewhere at the back of the place, its rapid knocking light and spiteful.

'*Morag!*' cried blind Harper, plucking helplessly at the dwarf.

Arm dragged him forward. His sight returned, but everything was reversed and tinted, fading at the edges. Morag was running ahead of them, clumsily.

He suffered a vision of Wendover – whom he thought he had known – as an insane stunted old man, his lips peeled wetly back, his eyes all yellow and black, shooting and shooting into a mass of bodies. 'We're all animals, Arm.' Expended shell cases spat over the old man's shoulder, his wasted body was braced against the kick of the gun. 'Just bloody well run!'

Villagers ran shrieking about under the machine-gun fire, their hands pressed to their eyepits, but they couldn't get away. Blood arced into the air from a ruptured skull, pumping abruptly to an unbelievable height. 'Bastards!' screamed the old man. *'Bastards!'*

Retching and gasping, Harper made it to the door.

Arm pushed him viciously into the cold night and he fell on the grass among old graves, shivering with terror and revulsion. Morag came, and pressed her long body against his; locked her arms and legs about him.

He clutched her, and rubbed his hands over her beautiful dirty face.

Wendover backed out of the church and dropped the exhausted machine pistol. His face was smeared and twisted; his hands were shaking. Harper pushed the girl gently aside and sat up.

'Doctor?' he called softly.

Wendover didn't hear.

Inside the building, Sister Dooley was shouting at her congregation. Arm went up to the doctor and said, 'Come on. Harper can travel now.'

Wendover glanced uncertainly round.

He shook his head.

'Where's the other thing. We haven't finished yet. You only used the magnesium,' he muttered. He looked pained and stunned.

'There's no need to do it, Doctor,' Arm took his elbow, as if to jerk him awake. 'We have all the time we need, as long as we go now. Come on.'

'*No!*' bellowed Wendover suddenly. He walked away from the dwarf, waving his hands, running them across his bald scalp.

'There are other considerations, now. We can't leave without . . . In there . . .' He covered his face. 'I want the other thing,' he said from between his fingers. He let his hands drop, but avoided Arm's eyes.

'No, Doctor. It isn't necessary. We've done the job.'

Wendover pulled out his revolver. He raised it and prodded it into the dwarf's face.

'*Give* it to me.'

Arm backed away.

'You're mad, Wendover. There it is.' He nudged something on the ground with his foot. Harper stood up to look at it, but couldn't make anything of it.

'There's no need for the gun,' said Arm. 'It's no

business of mine what you do. But don't weep at me afterwards. Don't do it!'

'What's the matter?' Harper pleaded. His earlier feeling that the world had now gone entirely mad, unable any longer to stand the psychic strain of the disaster, returned with new strength. He hurt and he just wanted to get away from the place. He thought that the nun wouldn't wait much longer before making some kind of counter-attack. 'Doctor! Arm, wait!'

Arm had turned on his heel and walked off into the darkness.

Wendover fiddled with the thing on the grass, picked it up. He turned on Harper a gaze of utter wretchedness, almost of astonishment. He stumbled to the door of the church and hurled the device inside.

The building shuddered and expelled a gout of flame from its east window.

A terrible cry went up from the congregation. Heat lashed out into the graveyard. Wendover staggered away from the door, his arms wrapped round his face.

Even the belfry dreamholes were full of fire. It spread at a terrifying rate. The rafters caught, the roof sagged. The doctor was whimpering and moaning.

His face obscured Harper's field of vision, twitching anarchically.

'How many of them in there?' it shouted.

Harper was going to be sick again. Saliva collected in his mouth.

Sister Dooley appeared in the doorway, her veil and habit cracking and burning. She rolled and jerked over the grass between the graves, waving her limbs.

Harper said: 'All of them. The whole village came. It was compulsory.' He went on his knees and retched bile up into his mouth, but it wasn't enough to relieve him.

Wendover nodded to himself several times. He choked and began to cry, wiping the sleeve of his raincoat across his eyes.

'Good,' he said, 'good. Oh my God.'

Arm was waiting for them on the road.

13: The Horse of the Mutant Queen

In the morning they made the final contact.

Wendover had called a halt, and the group was clustered about a small fire on the hard shoulder. Here, the motorway was on a level with its environs: on their left, twenty yards of scrub separated them from a conifer plantation; to the right, the crazed, cluttered expanse of the road, beyond which lay the empty concrete shells of manufacturing plant.

The ruins exuded a potent air of desolation, and though rain swept across the road in silver sheets, Wendover avoided the thought of taking shelter among the lifeless cubist forms. Grass grew from expansion slits in the concrete. A blue signboard eighty feet long read: L IS HO NIX IN. Rust stains crept across its surface.

Depressed, they huddled together as Morag gutted a rabbit. Arm poked about in its discarded entrails with a twig. Rain fizzled in the fire. Nobody had mentioned the doctor's berserk, and he was grateful. After the catharsis he had collapsed, and they had carried him some distance before halting for the night. There had been no pursuit.

He considered the desolate frontage of the factory, the colour of dried dung. He had lumped together all his recriminations and come clear through to the other side of them, into a deserted zone where acceptance was automatic. No single action or misjudgement of his compared to the first: to hang a meaningless, obsessive journey on a single act of misplaced pity; and then to implicate others in a trip through his own conscience. Something inbred compelled him to expiation: the child was a side issue at best, the piracy of the last few weeks nothing more than a corollary.

He tried to decipher the signboard, filling the gaps with letters chosen at random. Even the landscape was slipping away from him: he acknowledged only the road, even though it led to nowhere he hadn't been before.

He looked at the sleeping child. How does it feel to be a rationalization? he asked it. What's so different between my attitude to you and Sister Dooley's? We both needed you for something other than yourself.

There remained only the physical termination of the journey. After that, nothing would change.

'What do you think the signboard says?' he asked of nobody in particular. They were treating him very gently.

There was an argument about the meatier parts of the rabbit.

'Come off it, Arm,' said Harper, with grease dripping off his chin, 'who got it in the crotch last night?'

'It's favouritism. I expect you asked for it. We need a system, so everybody gets a chance at the good bits. Somebody ought to officiate.' He was joking, of course.

Wendover chuckled. He tore his meat up carefully, so it would be easier to chew. He put some pieces in his mouth and said, 'You got that in Tinhouse, um?' He sucked air in round the meat to cool it. He fished a bit of gristle from his mouth with a crooked finger. 'Um?'

It took a little time to realize they weren't listening, he had been so occupied with the food. He became aware of a faint musical sound.

'Doctor . . .' somebody said.

Twenty yards away, where the stiff olive and black gorse thickened and leaned against the bulk of the conifers, were gathered fifteen or sixteen mutants, the rain striking off their damp leathery hides.

He swallowed painfully and clambered to his feet.

They were milling silently about some hidden

focal point, paying little attention to the group
on the hard shoulder. He narrowed his eyes and
tried to see what it was. He coughed, he had
swallowed a sliver of bone. The apparently aimless shifting ceased; waist-high in the gorse,
they took up a line-abreast formation which
broke immediately to let the original figure of
their interest through.

Mincing unsteadily out of the conifers came
an emaciated pony.

A crude bitless bridle decked with small pieces
of polished tin and coloured plastic – the source
of the strange music – hung askew on the raw,
fiddle-shaped head. Wall-eyed and bemused,
ewe-necked and goose-rumped, it moved slowly,
skin alternately taut then sagging over big,
ungainly bones. Discoloured areas that might
equally have been filth or skin cancers showing
at stifle and withers. Its knees were bloody.

Some congenital deformity of the skull had
favoured it with an incipient horn, a short nub
of bone growing between its eyes.

On it sat an ancient, withered mutant woman.

Her hide was the colour of earth, coarse and
unsupple, resembling that of the child. Stiff
scaly wattles hung at each side of her jaw,
spoiling the spare lines of the oval head. On the
whole, she looked no different from the rest of

the tribe: the unreadable expression, the suggestion of a thoroughly alien attitude.

She brought the pony to a standstill and sat rigidly, regarding the humans with unnerving control and patience. Wendover felt no kinship: he could empathize nothing of what she must be feeling; whatever the circumstances of her birth, she was altogether something different.

The pony shifted its feet irritably. She checked it without fuss.

'Christ,' said Harper, 'is this what we came for?' But he sounded rattled. 'They never *say* anything.'

'Shut up,' Wendover told him. 'Where's the child?'

Morag was patently awed by the matriarch and her retinue. The baby woke and wailed hungrily. A ripple of motion passed through the rank of mutants.

Without looking at the girl, Wendover said, 'Give it to me,' intending to face her with what he had always presumed must be a painful decision. But the surgery seemed unnecessary: she settled it in his arms almost absently, still gazing at the regal old woman. And he found that his own voice had become petulant and nervy. Perhaps, he thought, I'm going to get involved even now.

'Walk forward slowly,' he ordered. 'And keep

your eyes open. We haven't any reason to suppose they like us very much.' He had become a wary expert, and it lessened him in his own eyes.

It was a long walk.

The gorse grew fingers and plucked at his raincoat. He stumbled over rabbit-holes and bits of metal flung off the motorway by old collisions. He was aware of Harper having the same difficulties – and Arm struggled like an out-of-temper goblin: his head hardly overtopped the bushes, and his round face, scarlet with exertion as he struggled with the spikes that snagged his rags, occasionally vanished completely.

'It's a circus,' panted Harper, although he had never seen one.

He had his arm possessively around the girl, helping her on. He had lost a rival and was elated; but Wendover felt only needles in his chest, the onset of weariness.

He seemed to be covering very little ground. The child complained and wet itself.

The old woman continued to regard them steadily; the pony ruminated over a mouthful of gorse, stupid and inert; the rain lashed spitefully at the sombre landscape.

The wind rose and played an oddly-pitched melody.

Pausing to untangle the skirt of the gabardine and hitch the child into a more comfortable position under his arm, Wendover discovered that it wasn't the wind at all.

Out of the corroded north of the motorway, coming through like a big, mad insect, shot a red turbine car. It was up in the high nineties. Gear changes batted back from the quiet wrecks.

Faced with a heavy twin-cabbed rig that blocked the south-bound carriageway, it drifted on to the central reservation; slewed past the obstruction; fish-tailed, accelerated madly and just as suddenly slowed. Wendover glanced at the others. They were watching its progress in silence.

It reached their fire, rolled over it, scattering embers and pulling up short with a creak of overloaded brakes.

It was a big, pathetic, ostentatious machine, one of the old Lewis/Phoenix Sunbirds. Rust stains raked the full length of its flamboyant body, like the clawmarks of a steel beast. Its cellulose was blistered, its chromed intakes knocked as crooked as the smile on the face of the tart. The back passages of its turbine clicked and contracted. A heat haze shimmered above its hood. A nearside window jerked stiffly open.

'I found you, Wendover!' called Holloway Ableson Pauce, as if it were all a complex but enjoyable game of hide-and-seek.

14: Destination Is A State Of Mind

'Mind you,' he continued, poking his massive head out of the window and wagging a knobby index finger at them, 'it wasn't easy, and I give you full credit for that. All that time grubbing about in that damn' city . . .' He withdrew his head abruptly (his aureole of silky hair was still bright and clean) and wound the window up. He fumbled for a moment with the door-catch, his face a fawn blur behind the dirty glass; then the door swung open and he slid out.

The lamé suit was tarnished and stained, ripped at the thigh, revealing soiled bandages. He now wore belt and holster outside his jacket, in lieu of buttons. His make-up had slipped – his features seemed to have run together like water-colour applied too wet to thin paper. Lumps of dirt had lodged in the cracks on his cheeks. He had lost a lot of weight since Tinhouse and he moved jerkily, like an insect.

He bent and rummaged in the car, reappeared

with a heavy gun, about three and a half feet long, black and oily and unpleasant.

Arm hissed quietly, eyes anxious.

Pauce lumbered through the scrub, resuming his monologue as he drew closer. His facial muscles flexed and came up with a smile. Bits of make-up fell from beneath his nose and eyes.

'I'm sorry about the shooting, Doctor. I was looking for medicine, for the leg . . .' He squinted at Wendover, his smile melting back into the mask. He was expecting something. 'Of course, you know about the leg. I *could* have killed you, you know. It was quite a shock seeing you there. But I merely took the medicine . . .'

It was retrospective applause he wanted. Nobody spoke. Wendover was exploring the novelty of the explanation: he went through the events in the surgery again, scoring off the stages at which he should have realized it had been Pauce who shot him, not some poor, mad denizen of Grocott Personnel's universe.

'You deserved it,' the mask snarled. Then, pointing the gun at the line of mutants and assuming a reasonable tone: 'I don't know what you're up to here, Wendover. But whatever it is, you do realize that in all conscience I can't allow it to go on.

'There are considerations of survival. Not just of you and I, or course . . .'

Abruptly the mask split open and a high,

metallic peal of laughter struck across the derelict landscape.

'I have *seen* them,' said Pauce. 'They are all
around us!'

Wendover couldn't remember which area of
the Midlands Pauce came from, but he had
always hated the accent: it was too well suited
to paranoia, its whine lent a wholly false
urgency to wholly false fears.

'You needn't worry, Pauce. They mean us no
harm.'

On the whole, he couldn't say that of Pauce.
He considered him with a good deal of fear and
nothing much at all in the way of compassion.
Remote eyes in cracked, desiccated hollows
stared back at him. I should have killed him
back in Tinhouse, he thought, but I was inexpe-
rienced then. He cast about for something else
to say.

Pauce waggled the gunbarrel at the mutants
again: glared at the old woman.

'Time is running against us,' he said. 'And
them. With the lapse of a generation or so we
shall be racially degenerate. It is only a matter
of time before the population becomes entirely
foreign.'

'Fuck off, Pauce!' Harper shouted suddenly.
'You're obsolete. Something is happening here
you'll never understand.'

Pauce ignored him. To Wendover, he said:

213

'Well, well. You've certainly broadened his mind, Doctor. Take care or he'll betray you too. You may not even have to feed him for twenty years to experience that privilege. Words, labels . . .' He turned savagely on the cripple. '. . . a *splendid* young parrot. An entertainment.' A rope of spittle quivered from his chin. He sucked it back in again.

'I'm afraid I'll have to ask you to put the child down, Wendover, and step away from it. This is quite like old times, dear me. Do you still have the revolver in your pocket? A dirty trick, particularly for a medical man: but I'm not likely to make the mistake a second time.

'Just move out of the way.'

His attention wandered to Morag, but nobody moved. He had them in a spell. He smiled pleasantly.

'I would close my eyes, young lady, if I were you . . .'

'Look, Pauce,' said Wendover. He saw the scene repeating endlessly, he and the golden man caught in a cruel temporal twist, playing out an archetypal scene. Again he experienced a terrifying feeling of impotence, of control over the environment lost. The inability to say anything new, knowing that the old things aren't going to work.

'Look, you must see. All this was worked out by the scientists during the disaster, perhaps

even before. These people are *designed* to live in
the world as it is. We aren't . . .'

'Not good enough, Doctor,' Harper broke in.
He came a pace forward. The parrot comment
had got to him. 'You have to know the right
words. Tell him about survival again, Pauce.

'Tell him about the dream of the Twentieth
Republic, and the new Tinhouse, stuff like that.

'Tell him about lost glories, achievements.

'Tell him, Pauce!'

Pauce swung his gun at the mocking voice. It
was plain that he wasn't seeing Harper, if anything. His mouth worked. His fingers writhed
over the trigger guard. An intension tremor
shook his huge old body.

'No!' cried Morag, darting forward.

'No!' cried Wendover.

The Smith & Wesson was stuck in his pocket.

Pauce's cannon roared and gabbled, its wicked
barrel flickering back and forth like the tongue
of some steel snake. It was designed to be
mounted in a mobile turret – Pauce's face contorted with pain as the recoil kicked it into his
hip. He stumbled about opening and shutting
his mouth. Struggling, the gun drove him back,
yard by yard. He stumbled, fell backwards,
regained his balance, went down on one knee.
He was moaning curiously, and every time the
gun went off the tone of his moan modulated,

like a boy tapping his larynx to imitate the cinema Indian.

On his knees, he mastered the gun, and a storm of fire took the girl and threw her down into the gorse. She lay in a tumbled mess, one leg kicking and kicking.

Small, shocked sounds crept into the silence: the hiss of the rain; the alarm call of a blackbird in the conifers; the rattle of a loose turbine-inspection plate.

Across the motorway, the signboard explained: L IS HO NIX IN.

Harper's hands made little vague motions. He had fallen down when the gun started up. He got up. He moaned and walked forward like a somnambulist.

He kept it up even when Pauce turned the cannon on him. His eyes remained steady, wide and aware. The repeated impact of the cannon shells made him stagger, but he stayed on his feet.

An odd thing happened.

Pauce leaned forward against the recoil. His expression shifted rapidly from hate to consternation. The cripple came on like a machine, swaying a little when his bad leg took his weight. The mechanisms of grief kept his eyes fixed on the cannon.

Pauce backed off one pace, then another: upright, he was barely in control of the gun.

He shut it down, bemused. Hammered at it with the heel of his hand, suspecting a failure. When he fired again, the gun took control energetically, firing at the vacant sky, trying to leap out of his hands.

Harper limped on, smashed and drunken. His eyes were narrowed, as if he wondered why the fight was abruptly between Pauce and the cannon.

But he didn't stop until he was confronting Tinhouse face to face, and it seemed that Pauce was the cornered one. Then he opened his mouth, and a great gout of blood spilled out. He fell on the barrel of the gun, tearing it out of Pauce's hands.

Arm ran forward, his voice a sudden, high-pitched wail.

Wendover ripped the lining out of the murderous pocket, extended his arm carefully, and shot Pauce through the head.

The golden man spun round and fell over, looking surprised. Something bright and silky and auburn flew off his head and fluttered down. The bullet had torn off his wig. His head was a broken yellow dome.

Wendover dropped the pistol. A frightening feeling seeped through his body and settled in his joints.

Smoke was drifting up from Harper's corpse. His reefer jacket had caught fire.

Forcing his rigid limbs to move, the doctor put down the screaming child and went to examine the rags of Morag. Nausea forced him to his knees by the wreck. He brought up the rabbit over her exploded head, shook and choked. He dragged himself to his feet, aware of the universe revolving once in a very long time. Images of the derelict factory whirled together with the face of somebody he had forgotten and the motionless line of unhumans. Concrete, flesh, flesh. The rain hissed. The inspection plate rattled.

Arm blocked his way as he headed blindly where Harper lay tangled up with the dreadful cannon.

Silly words marched rhythmically inside his skull. What every weevil knows. L IS HO NIX IN. He examined the sad face of the dwarf and asked, 'Arm, did you see which one of them she did it for?' Then he sat down and retched again, long spasms that did nothing to relieve the internal space.

'The child,' said Arm, after a pause, but he wasn't answering the question.

During the brief flurry of action the mutant woman had kept still, gazing impassively on and calming the pony when it shied at the cannon-fire. Possibly it had understood more than she had.

Now she kicked it forward. By Morag's body, it lowered its head. It stepped warily to one side, rolling its eyes, the abortive horn and runnels of fluid darkening the hair beneath its eyes lending it a grotesque air of surprise.

The woman regarded Arm and Wendover with a curious tilt of her head.

With a swift, precise motion, she hung off the animal's back and scooped the child out of the gorse. Upright again, she settled it on the pony's withers with no gentleness, and continued to stare. When it wailed, she rapped it decisively.

Wendover got up, using Arm's shoulder as a crutch. He met her alien eyes.

'Take the bloody thing away,' he said heavily. 'Just take it.'

The pony turned and stepped gingerly towards the conifers.

Wendover tried to look at Harper again, but the dwarf steered him carefully away.

'You can't help them, Doctor.'

'No, I lost my bag.'

Arm led him to the red turbine car, tactfully ignoring the tears that streamed down his senile face.

From the edge of the plantation she watched the vehicle whine into life and swing over the central reservation. When it had vanished into the north, she beckoned to the tribe. She urged the scrawny unicorn through the gorse past the corpses of the smooths. The tribe followed her across the road avoiding the collapsed hulks. She stopped before the incomprehensible sign-board, drew up her knees, and placed the child on her lap. They all stood looking at the trade-mark for some time. The rain stopped.

Epilogue

Nick Bruton, a spectre of the disaster, trudged a northbound route in some uncomfortable new boots he had got under odd circumstances. He suspected from the feel of it that he'd also picked up a dose in the last village.

The wind blew into his pale face and flapped his bottle-green jacket; his beautiful trousers were stuck to his legs, and his lace was damp.

In the villages they loved his lace and his singular ways, and though he didn't provide them with their answers, he never complained at the things they gave him. His ankle hurt a little. He whistled a small tune to himself and ran his hands through his splendid hair to see if it was dry. He hoped it wouldn't rain again for a while.

'I'm a highway child,' he sang, 'so don't deny my name.'

His peculiar chromosomes were good for another few years yet, and there was plenty to see. His destination was a state of mind.

Epilogue

It wasn't too often he heard a car on the road. This one was red. He stopped to watch it take a clear, sloping stretch, coming very fast, wallowing on its suspension. It was fortunate for him that before passing his present position it would be slowed down considerably by a battlement of wrecks. He stepped into the road, stretched out his arm, and jerked his long, powerful thumb.